DRAGON DEFYING

DRAGON DEFYING

DRAGON APPARENT™ BOOK FIVE

TALIA BECKETT

DISRUPTIVE IMAGINATION

This book is a work of fiction. All of the characters, organizations, and events portrayed in this novel are either products of the author's imagination or are used fictitiously. Sometimes both.

Copyright © 2023 Talia Beckett
Cover by Bandrei
Cover copyright © LMBPN Publishing

LMBPN Publishing supports the right to free expression and the value of copyright. The purpose of copyright is to encourage writers and artists to produce the creative works that enrich our culture.

The distribution of this book without permission is a theft of the author's intellectual property. If you would like permission to use material from the book (other than for review purposes), please contact support@lmbpn.com. Thank you for your support of the author's rights.

LMBPN Publishing
PMB 196, 2540 South Maryland Pkwy
Las Vegas, NV 89109

Version 1.00 February, 2023
ebook ISBN: 979-8-88541-780-8
Print ISBN: 979-8-88878-193-7

THE DRAGON DEFYING TEAM

Thanks to my JIT Team:

Christopher Gilliard
David Laughlin
Dorothy Lloyd
Diane L. Smith
Jan Hunnicutt
Zacc Pelter
Paul Westman

DEDICATION

To Bryan. You have stood by my side for a long time now and especially in the last year. I am honored to call you my partner in life. You show me the adventurous every day that we spend together and always have capacity for my emotions and the world inside my head.

It also helps that you don't seem to mind being woken up when I get ideas in the middle of the night and I'm too excited to go back to sleep until I've talked about them or written them down. Thank you for never being angry at me when I accidentally, or deliberately, wake you.

— Talia

CHAPTER ONE

Life on the yacht was more pleasant than I'd expected it to be. We'd slowed down, and for the first time in my life I was living as I wished, without the weight of anyone's expectations or any responsibilities.

I did still have things I was responsible for, but it wasn't the weight of a job, of paying bills to keep a roof over my head, of being the leader of a race reluctant to accept me, or the stigma of being a red dragon in a community that almost entirely hated red dragons. I could decide how I spent each day and progress in the manner I thought best.

It made me happier and helped me grow. Right now, I was putting that growth to the test, feeling for the shadow catchers nearby while I stood on the deck of the yacht and enjoyed the evening sun. I could smell the tantalizing scent of my mother's cooking. She'd also taken to being on the yacht and away from everything. This was more like the life she'd led before I'd found her.

Feeling the group of demons circling the area, I was pleased to note that there were still very few of them, but I was also disappointed. It meant they were learning to stay away from me, but it also meant fewer of them for target practice.

After coming to the yacht, Neritas had suggested we train by hunting nearby demons and sending them to their graves, and I loved the idea more than I had let on. It was a little dangerous, but our group was so used to fighting the creatures that we hadn't struggled. And it kept them back and gave me the satisfaction of doing something useful while I waited for everyone else to be ready.

Going to the gate a couple of weeks earlier had been tough and caused a huge fallout. I was still recovering from all the events around it, and I wasn't looking to go back just yet. But I couldn't ignore it forever. Alitas was giving me regular updates on the state of the gate using our markers.

The gate pillars were using up the extra energy I'd given them, and the circle of rot allowed by their weakening had grown back to almost the same place it had been. We couldn't go back without more dragons, something to help the pillars hold their charge, and a lot more preparation.

Jace was working with Elias to figure out how to repair and charge the pillars, a crucial element to our success. It was taking a long time, the knowledge surrounding them having been lost.

For some reason that no one knew for sure, the information in Detaris had been hidden or wiped. The young were not being taught the truth about the gate, and now they didn't realize how much they needed my unique skills. For now, I had to let that go, because there was no telling them they were wrong. And with any luck, though, I wouldn't need to. We were exploring other ways to get enough dragons together to recharge the gate.

Ben was gathering what information he could on red dragons and what we could do. The journal that Reijo had put together and left in the house trashed by the shadow catchers was information that he and my mother had collected and a few things he hadn't remembered or attempted yet that I'd already instinctively begun doing.

Everything else that red dragons could do was unnecessary, with technology the way it was, but still good to know it was possible for me. I flicked through Reijo's notes now and then and was considering doing so again this evening. It would occupy some time.

Despite all the positives, I was restless. I liked progress and, while the pressure was off, I was still sitting around waiting for more information and more allies. I wanted to do something, but on the last visit from Jace, I had been told to stay put.

The human world was also sneaking around and trying to find more evidence of dragons. The humans I'd saved on the way back from the gate the first time had talked despite promising not to. I was also still ignoring all my friends and my old boss, who had figured out that I was the warrior woman the world was calling to meet.

As I felt the shadow catchers' positions and tried to decide if I wanted to kill more of them or let them be, I noticed a change in their pattern. The one closest to the road slowed down and stopped, no longer rotating around the yacht and lake in the same pattern as the others. It could only mean one thing. Visitors of some kind.

Shifting slightly so I would be less visible from the road

to the lakeshore, I waited, and within a minute I saw a car approach. It was a familiar van. Friends had arrived, but I didn't know if they'd come with good news or not. This was not a planned visit.

My mind started to consider all the possible things that could have gone wrong since I last saw dragons from Elias and Sarai's group. I hoped they were all okay.

I didn't know whether to be relieved when I saw that it was Cios driving and Jace and Alitas both got out. They had another two dragons with them, and Kryos stepped out of the shadows of the tree line to join them as soon as they appeared.

Watching them and knowing it wouldn't be long until they were on the deck beside me, I wondered who the extra two dragons could be.

Kryos and Alitas talked for a few seconds before a couple more of my honor guards were waved over and one of them rushed to get the motorboat ready. Within another minute, all of them but Kryos were aboard and coming to me.

"Visitors," I called to the rest of the yacht, hoping at least one of them heard me and would get together some food and drinks to offer the newcomers.

It was a little lazy of me not to do it myself, but I wanted to focus on these two new dragons. I didn't recognize them from the farmhouse or Detaris, and Kryos didn't appear to have met them either, so they weren't gate guards. That left only one other possibility. They were dragons from another city.

Neritas appeared a few seconds later and stood by my side.

"Your mother is already happily laying out the good plates on the dining table and sent me to find out who we've got." He grinned.

I felt the corners of my mouth twitch before I tilted my head toward the boat. It was close enough that a single glance would be all he needed to take in who we had as well.

"New people," he simply said.

"Yup. No idea what they're here for. I can't imagine it will be long before we find out, however. Jace is usually to the point."

Neritas hurried back below decks, where my mom would already be worrying over what to feed them. There was plenty of food aboard, and now that life had slowed down again and she was able to focus on whatever she wanted, she had been cooking a lot with Reijo. Each night was another wonderful meal and there were always plenty of leftovers.

I got the feeling that it was what life had been like at the small farm she'd lived on before I'd come back into her world and taken her away. She was happier out here on the yacht than in Detaris.

"Good evening," I called when the motor boat was closer and Cios had slowed the engine, turning to come alongside more easily.

I moved to a section of the deck where I would be better placed to take a line thrown to me and helped them tether by a ladder up the back of the yacht. It took a moment to get them tied off and I was aware of the stares from the newcomers the whole time I did.

Alitas came up first, clearly looking for danger, and then Jace.

"You finally don't look like shit, Red," she said by way of a greeting.

I let out a chuckle as I shook my head. "Good to see you too."

"Let me introduce a couple of dragons to you. They've come over from a couple of dragon cities, one that hides out in Utah and another not far from there. They are eager to meet their first red dragon. Liam and Hiachi."

After shaking hands with them, I invited everyone below deck for refreshments and to get somewhere warmer. Not a person objected.

When we got down there, everyone but my mother was bustling around and finishing off laying the table and getting out drinks, and lighting candles to make the main saloon into an atmospheric dining area.

The table had several extensions that allowed it to accommodate a large number, and all of these had been used. It made it look almost opulent. This reminded me of some dragons' kindness and I made a quick comment about how grateful I was to Jace and her team for housing us on the yacht.

As we all sat to eat, we made small talk, introduced everyone, and talked about life away from a city.

"I miss flying. We've not dared to fly outside of a city and the veil after everything the human world has noticed," I said as most of us were finishing up.

"You're welcome to head down to our city for a visit sometime. I think there are a lot of us who are eager to see a red dragon in the flesh. Jace has been telling us that you can really fly," Hiachi said.

"Not sure I'm that amazing, but I try my best. I'd love to visit another city though. As I'm sure the rest of us would."

"The more the merrier. And that's why we're here. We've known Cios from when we were kids. He told us that the gate needs attention and is getting weaker. That you need as many dragons as possible to help."

"Yes, very much so. But I won't lie, it's also dangerous." I met his gaze as he studied me, hoping to prove to him that I was sincere. As much as I wanted their help, I wanted them to understand what that meant.

Not everyone could handle the pressure or the walk to the gate, let alone everything else that could happen. The voices in their heads could be another very real danger.

After the last trip, I had confided in some of the others that I could hear the creature beyond the gate. It turned out I wasn't the only one, although not all of us could. Neritas and my mother had also heard him speak and had to ignore the jibes and comments designed to stop them.

I was curious why only the three of us had been targeted but could find no obvious reason, so I'd let it go. I had more pressing matters. For the next few minutes, I talked about the gate and the obstacles to powering it up again.

Our visitors listened, waiting until I was done before they thought about it and talked to each other in quiet voices we couldn't quite hear.

"Neither of us will deny that it sounds like a challenge that not every dragon would want to take on. Not without some assurances, or a lot of powerful dragons there to protect them. Maybe even a partially strengthened gate. Or at least as much as it can be powered up without more help."

"We're honestly hoping that we will have several more dragons volunteer to help us to attempt to strengthen it in stages. If you wanted to stagger any offered aid to safety levels, that would fit right in with our thinking already. But we need more help to begin the process. My group isn't large enough to even get to the gate and back safely currently."

"That's quite the problem."

"It is, but I won't risk their lives taking them there unless I can be sure we can bring them back."

"Hearing that definitely helps." It was the first time Liam had spoken, and it gave me the impression that he was the more cautious of the two and the one tempering their response.

"I know I'm asking a lot. It's not something I would expect anyone to decide on without hearing more, being able to discuss it, and seeing who volunteers. I wouldn't want anyone to feel forced into helping me. With that said, the world is depending on us to find a way to fix and power this gate. I will need some help."

"And the dragons of Detaris aren't interested in doing any more to help?" Hiachi asked.

"They got scared," Griffin put in. "I am one of the elders, and they kicked me out rather than allow me to show them the proof I have. They wish to act as if a red dragon isn't needed on the throne and as if they are holding the fort perfectly well for the rest of our kind."

Hiachi leaned forward, getting my attention. "I won't

deny, they have also recently communicated with our city leadership and they have informed us that they don't recognize your claim to the throne and won't support you. What makes you convinced that you're the queen we should be following?" Hiachi asked difficult questions and opinions, and I appreciated his honesty.

"I don't want to be your queen necessarily. If people choose to put me on that pedestal, I cannot stop them, and several of the dragons before you think that it will involve me claiming a throne at some point, but it's not my main goal. I want to get the gate fixed and powered back up. After that, who knows." I shrugged as I looked between the two dragons and picked up on the vibe they were giving off. They weren't very impressed with anything I was saying right now.

"You know she's also been to the island of Kilnar, and the ancestors have blessed her. She is the rightful heir." My mother sat forward, and she seemed to have spoken the right words. They were followed by a stunned silence.

"I've never been sure the rumor was real," Hiachi replied.

"It's real," my mother insisted. "I've been there many times. Her father, the last king, took me, and now I've taken her."

Hiachi and Liam bowed toward my mom, looking mortified that they'd not realized who she was sooner. I fought back a grin as they tried to grovel and make it right.

"We're sure that if all of you came to our cities and told our elders everything we've heard this evening, they'd at least ask our stronger dragons if they wished to help."

"That would be more than enough. We just want to get

the news out there and see who feels they can offer some help. We accept your invitation." I smiled, feeling like I might finally be making some more progress.

I glanced over at Jace and caught her smirking, her eyes glinting at what was happening, and knew she deserved the satisfaction of feeling like she'd made this happen. She'd gone a long way to find us a potential ally or two, and I was more than grateful.

CHAPTER TWO

Waking up finally felt as if it meant something. I sprang up out of bed, pulled clothes on in a hurry, and shuffled from my bedroom on the yacht to find the glorious smell of bacon wafting from the galley and the sound of quiet voices in the dining area.

With my stomach growling at the prospect of good food and curiosity to get to know our visitors more before we worked out our plans, I padded in that direction.

Neither of our guests were up yet, but our usual crew was, except for Cios and some of the gate guards who were off duty and making the most of a warm bed and safety. Other times, they had to sleep rough and not far from demons, so I couldn't fault them for wanting to sleep in on occasion.

After helping myself to a plate from the buffet, where Reijo was adding more bacon, I sat between Flick and Neritas, the pair always leaving me a seat between them.

"Sounds like you're all talking about something important," I said, noticing that they'd stopped the moment they saw me.

Although I wondered if they had been talking about me, I doubted any of them had a problem telling me what they thought of me. I did not want them to stop talking if it was anything else. Food only needed so much of my attention.

"We're discussing if we should all go to this city. And whether you should take the risk or stay here." Ben got to the point, making it clear that the conversation was a bit of both of my assumptions.

"I don't want to stay here a moment longer than I have to," I replied, then winced. "Don't get me wrong. I like it on this yacht. It's been amazing to chill out here for a while. But I need to see if I can get us allies and find out how others respond to a red dragon. Part of me needs to know if I'm going to face the same rejection I did in Detaris. And as much as I know you would all do a good job if I didn't go, if there's any chance that me being there will help, I can't stay here just to keep safe."

"That's the kind of thing your father used to say." My mother came from the kitchen carrying a platter of scrambled eggs. She placed it down and joined us to eat. "And he was often right. But even when he wasn't, he learned something important. So you have my vote to go. For what that's worth."

"Thanks, Mom." I reached for a one-armed hug as she moved past me to another empty seat.

"Just make sure I can come with you. I'm tired of being left behind."

That earned a chuckle from most of the table. Everyone continued to eat in silence for a few minutes, and I wondered if the discussion was over already. I'd stated what I wanted to do and no one had objected strongly, but Alitas didn't look entirely happy. He gazed off into space as he thought, and I could only wonder what was on his mind as I studied him for a few seconds.

"Is there any other way to do it?" Neritas asked. "We don't know how dangerous the journey will be. If the demons try to follow you, you'll need us."

Frowning, I considered this possibility. Neritas was right. I had no idea if the shadow catchers were going to keep plaguing me. What if they did follow me and try to attack wherever we stopped?

"Are the other cities protected? If we led shadow catchers to them, would dragons get hurt?" I asked.

"That's a good question," Jace replied. She was the only person at the breakfast table who had been to any of the other cities, as far as I was aware. Although I suspected Alitas might have.

"I think Liam's city should be fine. Hiachi's is another matter." Alitas confirmed what I suspected. Jace nodded along.

"I haven't seen Liam's. He was in Hiachi's when I got that far." Jace took a quick drink before tilting her head to the side. "I'd agree with Alitas on Hiachi's city. It's not well protected compared to Detaris. It's never needed to be. It's out in the desert, and I don't think there's anything that would stop the creatures, other than the lack of water. But Liam's is more like Detaris. He told me it floats on the great salt lake."

"Near Salt Lake City?" I'd always wanted to see that part of the world.

Jace grinned as Alitas gave me an affirmative.

"No telling her that she's not going now," Reijo teased with a smile.

"We'll go to Liam's then, and if that goes well and we don't think that the shadow catchers followed us, then we can go to Hiachi's as well." I hoped it sounded like a sensible plan, but Jace frowned.

She leaned in a little and kept her voice low. "I got the impression that they really want you to go to both cities. I don't think they'll like favoritism."

"So just tell them we will. If we think Red is going to be in danger, we change our plans." Flick shrugged as if this was obvious.

I saw their logic, but I wasn't on board with not mentioning that something might derail our plans if we couldn't be sure it was safe. It wouldn't be good for anyone's morale if we went back on what we'd said.

I shook my head after only a few seconds of thinking.

"No. Whatever we tell them we'll do, I want us to be honest about it. And I'd like to try and visit both cities if possible. I think it's only fair if they've both come all this way and gone to the effort to hear me out here. We'd want someone to give us the same courtesy."

"If I'm not happy that it's safe, I'm going to speak up," Alitas insisted. "I don't have a backup escape route down there."

"That makes it sound as if that tunnel from the gate isn't a one-off." Jace looked at the honor guard as if he was craftier than she'd realized and she respected it immensely.

While I didn't like the suggestion that I needed rescuing, it made me wonder what else he had up his sleeve.

Instead of admitting anything, he kept a neutral face and shrugged.

Ben said, "Okay, on that very mysterious note, I'm with you, Red. We should be truthful and honest with these guys but make it clear that, while we really want to go to both cities, if we don't deem it safe we'll try and find another way. That we'll work with them if we can." He sat back and folded his arms as if this settled the matter.

I fought back a smile. He'd been a father figure, protecting me since the beginning of my life as a dragon, and he still had a big say in my life. For a while, it had irritated me, but now I saw it for what it was: an expression of his care and desire to finish what the love of his life had started. He had been devoted to Anthony, and it turned out that Anthony had been a secret honor guard of sorts to the royal family.

Alitas had known he was in service to the king, but not to whom he answered directly. And Reijo knew he had been assigned to watch out for me, but again, not by whom. Reijo had set up the financial fund for me and had been paying into it my whole life, but he had been directly instructed to do so by the king with money the king had given him to get the whole project going.

We still had no answer on whom Anthony had been reporting to or gathering information for, and we hadn't been able to translate and decode massive chunks of his journal. Ben had decoded a few pages near the end out of order, hoping they might bring us some early clues, but they spoke almost exclusively of his fear that I might have been discovered and it was possibly about to come to an end. I didn't like the sound of that any more than Ben had.

Of course, as far as we were aware, I'd dealt with that threat. But we still needed answers. I had begun to suspect that we would never get them and never translate the whole thing, but Ben had promised that he wouldn't give up.

Over the next half an hour we all polished off a lot more food and waited for our guests to join us. I talked to my mother about where she had followed my father and asked her if I was going somewhere he had been.

Sometimes it was painful to hear everything that they had been able to do together. I wished I had known them both and not been hidden from the only community I could truly call family. But this time, my experience traveling would be something I might be able to imagine my father doing.

Over the next half hour, my friends drifted away. They had nothing more to add and they were used to waiting for someone else to figure out our fate.

Eventually, our guests woke up and shuffled through for breakfast and coffee. The rest of the guards appeared at a similar time, and Hiachi flinched away slightly.

"It's okay," I assured him. "They're off duty. It can be tough out there, facing shadow catchers day after day."

"I'm not used to seeing so many stern dragons who are dressed for battle," he explained as he accepted an empty plate from me. I pointed out the small buffet. It wasn't as hot as it had been, and they would be two of only a few still eating, but it was better than nothing and they beamed with excitement.

"The kit is an important part of why we're safe." I spoke

while my brain tried to remember what I needed to tell them and get it out so it made some sense.

Neither guest replied until they had food, and I had to rethink what I wanted to ask and say. Why did all these difficult conversations always fall to me?

"Okay, after sleeping on everything and having a talk with Alitas and my honor guard, we've decided that the best thing to do is have my entire group travel with me. I know that's a lot of people—"

"Oh, we expected that you'd have a fair amount with you if you were who Jace said. A queen is going to have all sorts of people around her." Liam smiled as if this settled the matter.

I sat back, feeling some of the tension leave me. I'd expected them to think I was being crazy and demanding, a prima donna of some kind. Instead, they seemed to be amused and almost happy at the idea of me bringing a large entourage.

Although I didn't understand the reasoning behind their enthusiasm, I was grateful, and their acquiescence to my first need made me feel bolder about the second.

"My safety is of concern to Alitas as well, and he feels that having plenty of the dragons with me who are used to fighting demons will aid us considerably in keeping us safe."

"I believe my city has resources they can also grant to aid in this manner," Liam replied as if this was nothing troublesome.

I thanked him as Hiachi shifted.

"Safety and guards are not something my city is as

readily able to pledge, but I do know they would be willing to work with Alitas to satisfy him in any way necessary."

"That is what I was going to come to next. We have found that the demons find me easily, and only water seems to hold them back indefinitely. While we wish to visit both cities, we may have to have a very fine-tuned plan to visit your city, Hiachi. I don't want to endanger the dragons there, even if I can handle the demons."

"I understand. As I said, my elders are eager to do what they can."

"Perfect. Then I hope that we can find a way to make that happen safely. We'll do what we can. I'm excited about it."

My final words made the two dragons the happiest I'd seen them, and I spent the next few minutes asking them about their cities, customs, cultural differences, or anything else that I might want to be aware of.

I wasn't sure what had made me think of it, but the questions I asked also added to the good-natured friendship forming as I listened to them describe their homes and anything I might need to know. They didn't sound different from other cities, with the exception that the inhabitants were dragons.

Both cities had the same veils that Detaris did, and they were out of the way where humans wouldn't easily find them. It was pretty typical protection. They sounded smaller and as if they had fewer elders, but that the elders liked to be involved in whatever was going on.

"There's a large tower on one side of the city," Liam said. "A suite there will be made ready for you. It hosted your father once, and I think they're eager to see it used again."

I grinned as I thought of the same thing in Detaris and how familiar and homey it had been. The more we talked, the happier I felt. After so long having everyone but honor guards and my friends react to me with anger and distrust, it would be nice to not be hated anymore.

As if some part of my brain couldn't be happy, however, it reminded me that I shouldn't get too used to it. It wouldn't help to get a big head from any of this. The most important thing was finding some allies, dragons willing to face the dangers of the gate and the demons helping to guard it.

Time would tell if I gained any of those.

CHAPTER THREE

Relief flooded through me as we got on the road again. We'd been driving for a few hours, and I was enjoying it more than I expected.

Once again we were in a convoy, and I was sitting between my two favorite people in the back of a car Alitas was driving. Ben had been demoted to a passenger, but he didn't seem to mind. It allowed him to focus on other things, like telling me anything and everything I might need to know and pointing out signs of wildlife along the way.

We'd just stopped for a late lunch in a small town along the route and had been there long enough that I'd started to feel some shadow catchers draw near. They were cautious, almost pack-like, and didn't behave like the shadow catchers by Detaris and the gate. But they'd grown bolder as we'd sat in one place for longer, and I didn't want a fight today.

Although Liam and Hiachi had come to the yacht with

almost the sole purpose of bringing me back with them, they had gone on ahead with Cios and Tim and Harriet to make sure the cities knew I was coming and the vague plans we'd made.

I tried not to worry about the reception I would get, but I'd begun to consider it. Would any of them hate me the same way the dragons in Detaris did? Or would they all be excited to meet a red dragon? Liam and Hiachi had confirmed that, other than my father, there hadn't been a red dragon in the area in a very long time.

It was strange to think about there being so few when all the other colors were in good supply. More than once I'd pondered why, and I'd asked Ben. Neither of us had a good answer.

The miles ticked by as we went north and toward the large lake we would be visiting first. It was exciting to visit somewhere new, and surrounded by the dragons I was comfortable with, I felt as if we were going on vacation.

"There's the lake," Ben said when he spotted it before anyone else.

Although he pointed, it took me a moment to realize the splotch on the horizon was the lake. It was a sight that grew over the next little while until we were driving down the side of it and I was sure Alitas would drive us off the edge of the road onto something that looked as if it were nothing but water and we were heading to our deaths.

"Hmmm. I can't remember exactly where the entrance to this city's veil is," Alitas said a few seconds later, slowing the car a fraction as he did. "I hoped I would recognize it, but it was so long ago that it's changed too much."

"Just head on past a bit slower than normal and see if we spot anyone familiar or if someone comes running out of nowhere behind us to try and get our attention." Ben shrugged. His suggestion wasn't bad, but he wasn't a lot of help.

"Could we get someone to come out to us or message ahead to Cios maybe?" I didn't like the idea of driving off the visible path and hoping it didn't offend them rather than spur them on to rescue us. Misunderstandings had been caused by less.

"That might be worth it," Alitas agreed.

Before any of us could attempt to contact anyone, Ben pointed to a couple of people sitting by the side of the lake. They glanced up at our cars, taking them in and pointing at us a few seconds later.

"Is that Liam?" Ben asked when the two men got up.

"I think so," I replied. "Can't hurt to slow a little more and see if they try to wave us in somewhere. It looks like there's a wider section of road there."

Alitas slowed a bit more and pulled forward. When we were still a hundred yards or so ahead of them, it became obvious the two men were waiting for us. One of them was Liam and the other wore something similar to the guards in Detaris and carried a shield. They moved apart and stood purposefully on the edge of the road, motioning for us to drive between them.

Grateful for their forethought, I waved at them as soon as I thought they would see. Both men bowed and then we were past them and heading out into what looked like the edge of the lake.

As Alitas took a short drive of faith, the view before and around us shimmered and morphed into what was truly there. The lake before us became a solid causeway, the road going out much farther into the water.

Similar to Detaris, there was a small section for parking cars and a road heading into the city. Unlike Detaris, this wasn't solid land and could also be disconnected from the land, leaving the parking lot floating along with the rest of the city.

Another big difference between the cities was how tall all the buildings were and how they were tethered. It looked as if the entire city could float and travel if need be.

On the other side of the veil, Alitas slowed again, but more dragons came forward in human form and waved us ahead. I noticed there weren't many in the air in dragon form, and the few who were weren't doing any particularly fancy flying. It was still another dragon city, however, and I could appreciate the epicness of seeing a dragon of any color as it soared through the air.

Alitas pulled into one of several spaces. Only two others were there already, and one of them was the car Cios usually drove., I wondered whether there were dragons out of the city for one reason or another or if they only had one vehicle, but I didn't get to think about it for long or ask anyone I was with if they had any thoughts one way or another.

We'd arrived, and that meant I had to greet a whole bunch of dragons and try to impress them enough that they'd join us.

Neritas reached back to help me out as soon as he was

on his feet outside the car. Hoping Flick didn't mind, I took the offered hand and got out.

There was applause and cheering as I stood and straightened, then dragons flew around us as if they were doing a brief aerial display. I watched them as the rest of the cars in our convoy pulled up to form a row beside mine and more and more dragons got out.

With Alitas and his honor guard, my friends and family, Jared and Griffin, who had tagged along to learn and hope to not repeat the failures of Detaris anywhere, and Jace and her crew, we had five cars and they each had at least four people.

The guards formed up around me protectively, but not so close that they'd prevent anyone sincere from talking to me. I tried not to worry about them being there and instead focused on moving toward the nearest dragon who looked at me with intent. It was an elderly man with a cane held in one hand and a stoop to his body that I would struggle to live with.

"Good evening, Scarlet." He spoke slowly and bowed as he did. "Welcome to the city of Trellian."

"Thank you," I replied. "I hope this is the first of many visits. And thank you for agreeing to let me come to your city and talk to your elders."

"I'm Valkin, our chief elder, and I have prepared the suite for you and your friends. The closest buildings have also been made available for your guards and the other people aiding you."

Once again I expressed my gratitude as I was led toward the building. It felt strange to be walking on a floating surface, almost as if the city was a giant ship and wobbled underfoot in a similar manner. It took me a little while to get used to it, even after being on the yacht, and I wondered if I appeared to be drunk in the meantime.

As we went, others came to wave and say hello. A lot of them were shy, and no one dared to keep us from proceeding. When we were still about a third of the way from the building that would be our home for the next few days, a young male ran up and handed me a flower.

Without really thinking, I took it and sniffed it before carrying on again. It wasn't anything I recognized. The purple petals and leaf shape were not a combination I'd seen before. The scent was sweet and aromatic, however, and I tucked it into the pocket of my jacket.

This made the young man smile before he slipped back into the masses of bodies and I was forced to concentrate on what was ahead of me again. I smiled anyway, and before long someone appeared with another.

Not wanting to show favoritism, I took this one as well and added it to the pocket with the first. Once again, I got a positive reaction, but the dragon didn't back away, and Neritas struggled to squeeze past on that side to make the dragon back up.

By the time another few minutes had passed and I was still slowly walking through the city, more young dragons came up to me, each one holding out gifts. Mostly it was trinkets, beautiful stones, gems, or something they'd crafted, like a small wooden toy. I tried to take all these as well, thanking everyone, but I had no idea what to do with all of it.

When it got to the point that I couldn't carry anything

else and I could barely move forward as so many came up with gifts, I looked at Ben for help.

"As wonderful as it is that everyone wants to greet Scarlet personally and present her with gifts, perhaps we could encourage everyone to do so a bit later and have a very specific moment for it? Something that includes dinner, perhaps?" Ben looked pointedly at Valkin, hoping the elder would step in and calm his city down so we could keep moving.

"I'm sure that could be arranged." The elder tried to get his guards to keep the crowds back and let me through.

Not sure how else to let people know that I would stay if I could but that I was very tired, I yawned. It started as a fake one, but by the time I was done, it was a real display of exhaustion.

Thankfully, a little encouragement from the guards and my body language was enough for people to let me through again, and I finally made the last section of the walk to the building on the far edge of the city. After everything else, I was faced with several flights of stairs. I wanted to curse them, but they were enclosed and I was finally going to be out of the eyes of the public.

Although I had a wooden goblet in one hand and a necklace clutched in the other, I still managed to wave to everyone behind me before I ducked inside and followed Valkin upward.

Even in all these crowds, Alitas had never lost his cool. My guard had kept close to me, kept me moving, and seen me safe so far. It was a good sign that he was used to this, even if I wasn't.

Waiting in the suite were several other people. A

woman stepped forward and smiled as she gave me a curtsy.

"Welcome, Princess. I and my team will look after all your needs. If anything isn't to your satisfaction, please don't hesitate to ask."

I smiled at her and tried to remember my manners, but as I tried to thank her for her help and shake her hand, the carefully balanced stack of gifts I was holding slipped, and several items fell to the floor.

I bent over to pick them up and more fell until I was barely holding anything, and I noticed that in the chaos and the overwhelm of gifts, I had accidentally crushed the original flowers in my pocket.

"It's been a long day," I offered to explain my clumsiness and lack of decorum.

I noticed the corner of her mouth twitch up.

"Let us leave you to settle in a few minutes and then we'll show you to dinner and make sure you'll have everything you need until morning."

"That sounds perfect. Thank you," I replied as Neritas and Flick put down the gifts they had collected for me and helped pick up the others.

I tried to smile at all the others who were there, another woman and two men standing off to one side at the moment. I wasn't sure what their roles were, but I made the mental note to introduce myself to all of them personally when they returned in a few minutes.

It was strange to look through the building as I was directed to my room, finding several plush bedrooms with large, comfortable-looking beds along the way. There weren't enough for everyone, but Alitas did a swift look-through with a couple of his guards and they had a quick chat before Alitas assigned the rooms to us.

"For maximum safety and ease of us protecting you," he explained when I lifted my eyebrows at the notion of being told where to sleep.

"You anticipate trouble?" I asked when everyone else had moved off. He was still with me as I put down my pack and considered what to pull out. Once again, I had put everything that mattered to me inside my rucksack, along with a change of clothes in case the worst happened. I had more clothes and toiletries in another bag, but I hadn't been the one to carry it and I didn't know where it was right now.

"I'm hoping there won't be trouble, but it's my job to be prepared for it and to make sure you're safe. Red dragons have had a rocky past. Some have come to harm on trips like this. I don't think you have anything to worry about, but that's my job to figure out too."

I exhaled and thought about this as I sat on the edge of the bed. "Is there anything I should be aware of to help keep me safer?"

"Don't eat or drink anything without checking with me or whichever honor guard I've put in charge at that moment. I'd try not to make it obvious, but if you look at us, we'll give a nod if it's safe."

I gulped as Alitas thought for a moment. This had come off the top of his head. I'd never considered that someone might want to poison me, but I guess that was something monarchs had to worry about.

"Try not to get separated from us. And definitely not from Flick and Neritas. Those two would die for you and have been with you since the beginning. If you have anyone's loyalty you have theirs, and that can mean more than you know. But...this isn't advice for now, as such, but be careful with them. They both feel for you and I know that you haven't thought about romantic attachments yet. Neither is red, and while I would never tell you what to do in matters of the heart, if you're unkind or lead either on, you could turn one of them from the most loyal friend to someone who hates you and would do anything to ruin your future."

I shuddered at the words Alitas said. It sounded awful, but it was the sad look in his eyes that gave me the most concern. Had he seen something like this before?

Hesitating to ask cost me the opportunity, as the two dragons in question reappeared. Alitas had assigned them the closest room together. They didn't seem to mind sharing, and I studied them both now. They were unlikely friends and had bonded over their joint mission to protect me when everyone else in the city had shown me animosity.

Alitas left once they settled his sleeping arrangements while he knew I was safe.

I looked at them both as they smiled at me.

"Thank you." I made sure to give them both as much eye contact as I could. "You two have given up a lot for me and put yourselves on the line many times. I want you to both know that you mean a lot to me. Both of you."

"We get it, Red. Don't sweat it. You're going to be queen someday, no matter what the idiots in Detaris say, and we're coming along for the ride. We've got your back just like you've got ours."

Although Neritas spoke, I could see the light in both of their eyes. They were in agreement and I knew that whatever they had said between them about me when I wasn't there, they had a definite bond. They were in this with me, exactly as Alitas had promised they would be.

CHAPTER FOUR

It was strange to be collected for dinner, but I took the opportunity to finally introduce myself to the dragons assigned to us and made sure that they knew I was grateful. I needed everyone to like me if nothing else.

We were taken to a nearby building with a large dining area already laid out for my friends and me. We were asked for our names and shown to set tables as if it were a formal dinner at a wedding. It threw me off at first, but I tried to roll with it.

Although I didn't know where the organizers had gotten their information from, someone must have told them who was important, because Neritas, Flick, Ben, my mother, and Reijo were kept with me while everyone was assigned to other tables. We had empty seats opposite all of us, and I noticed several at every table.

Alitas and several other guards were nearby, with one at each table. He sat himself down in such a way that I would always be able to have direct eye contact with him if I needed it and no one would block him from seeing me. If

I knew nothing else of the arrangements, I knew he'd had something to do with it and I marveled at how much he thought of that I hadn't considered.

Before long, more dragons appeared, and they filed in as if they already knew where they would be sitting. Valkin was at the table with me, along with the other elders from the city.

I introduced my table to them and Valkin introduced the rest to us while drinks were served. I was given water and offered a variety of other drinks.

I glanced at Alitas before giving a response to the question. He was looking my way and paying attention, but he didn't give any indication that he knew I might be checking for the safety of the options. In the end, I ordered a soda and declined anything alcoholic. If nothing else, I wanted to have my wits about me.

The drink was served in less than a minute, and as I was handed it, I looked at Alitas again. This time he was looking my way and he gave me a subtle nod.

Instantly relaxing, I took a sip and put the cup down where I would always be able to see it. As a woman, I'd learned never to take my eyes off my drink once I'd got it. You just couldn't go anywhere in LA without taking that precaution.

We made small talk about the accommodation and the city at first, and I did my best to be polite, though I wanted to move away from formalities and get to the important things, like why I was there. But I wasn't sure what the etiquette was. What was a princess meant to do or say at these sorts of things?

I tried not to worry about it as a starter of shrimp was

served, and once more I checked with Alitas that I could go ahead.

The elder opposite me, a woman who looked as if she had seen more years than anyone else I'd ever met, caught my gaze going in that direction and also looked that way briefly.

"Ah, you have many taking care of you and keeping you safe. This is good. I know it won't do much to reassure you now, but you are safe here, and given enough time, I'm sure we can prove so to yourself and your honor guards. In the meantime, I hope it doesn't cause you too much stress and difficulty."

Her concern made me smile but she was right. I wasn't so trusting as to believe everything that was said to me anymore. After Capricia seemed so supportive of everything I was doing then swung so wildly to the other extreme, I didn't trust words alone. Capricia had watched me getting attacked and did nothing, ignoring her duties as city guard captain. But that wasn't something I could easily explain here and now.

It seemed lame to just thank this elder, but another elder leaned in and rescued me.

"I must say, I think you're doing well with having not only so many good-looking young men around you but also plenty of strong women. It's clear that you're a good leader from the number and variety of dragons already at your side. I was very pleased to see you all arrive and observe the easy manner between you. And I remember your mother from seeing her in another city with your father. I think sometimes it bothered the king, but your mother had the same easy manner and likability."

"I just try to treat people like people and be the best I can be. It's not easy to get along with everyone, but I try."

"You have fought alongside all of these dragons as well, have you not?" Valkin asked.

"Yes. I've been constantly hunted by the shadow catchers, and some came with handlers as well. We have fought many times and some of my crew have risked their lives to see others safe, including me. I know I can trust them with my life and they know the rest of us have their backs too. No matter what our intentions may be, our actions have already said everything they need to."

"Then your bond makes me envious. As does the excitement of the plans you are working on. Although these old bones would struggle with such adventures now."

"With any luck, we can make the world safe enough that none of you would ever need to fight again, and the adventures we can all go on are a little less dangerous."

"Diplomatically put," the elder replied with a chuckle.

"You're hoping to defeat the demons? Will they then be gone completely?" the original elder asked, her voice rising in pitch as she did.

I shook my head.

"I don't know if something like that is possible. The gate has definitely weakened, however, and I'm sure that the increased activity of the demons and their handlers is in part because of this. If we can strengthen the gate, then I think we can send more of them back and reduce the numbers again."

"Red here is becoming quite the demon hunter. It's almost a sport for her when she's bored." Flick grinned, and I wasn't sure whether to join him or not. I was grateful that he'd spoken highly of my fighting skills but didn't want the focus on me.

"How does it work, to fight them? What do you need to do to kill one?" Valkin asked as we finished the first course and the plates were taken away to make room for the next.

I spent the time in between courses explaining how red dragons could bring the magic together and focused on how it was a team effort. It wasn't easy to explain simply, but I did my best.

They had lots of questions but also showed understanding quickly, making it a breeze to talk to them. It wasn't long before I could turn it back to the conversation about the gate and how, as a red dragon, I played a big part in powering that up as well.

"It sounds as if there's a lot of pressure on your shoulders, especially for one so young. You must find it difficult to have to give so much of your life to protecting others."

I thought about the question. I wasn't used to getting such understanding from anyone outside of my closest friends, or any empathy, and for a moment the genuine concern caught me by surprise. This wasn't what I was used to.

"There is some pressure, but I lost a dragon who was very important to me before I learned of my powers. He had been keeping me safe. There's a part of me that is more than eager to honor his legacy and save others from the same pain. I want us to all be safe."

This seemed to end the conversation as the elders gave me their condolences and we continued our meal. Having already told them some of the reasons why I was there, I didn't try to push any harder or bring it up again, instead letting my mom ask about the city and the life there.

It was my turn to listen as they talked about the challenge of running a city that was in such a difficult place that, while easily hidden, was not so easily provided for. Because they couldn't easily grow much food and the area was so heavily Mormon and integrated as a culture, they couldn't easily go and buy food in bulk or grow it and bring it to the city to swap without getting questions and curiosity. They were outsiders and different, yet local and here to stay.

That meant their food and provisions had to often be shipped in more covertly, cost more, and required careful planning.

"I won't deny that seeing the videos of your exploits in the human world made us wonder what it would be like if the human race knew of us and we no longer had to hide. It is not the same task it was when I was first an elder. The humans are expanding and coming up with technology at an alarming rate now."

"Do you think that we will be able to keep it from them much longer?" Valkin asked the question as innocently as he could, but he leaned forward and studied me, betraying his interest in the answer.

I wasn't sure it was a question I could easily answer. I didn't want to keep the existence of dragons hidden either, but we couldn't know how humanity would react. Keeping it a secret was getting harder as humanity continued to spread out, and I wondered if other cities were also struggling.

I decided to answer honestly. "I don't know. Humanity

is hard to predict and there's no way to know what will happen once the gate is powered back up."

"Do you think they deserve to know finally? If they'd accept an explanation now that they have come so far as a race?"

It was another impossible question to answer, but it mirrored the logical path my thoughts had taken. What I took most from their questions was their desire for the answers. Although they were trying to look as if it didn't matter, they were all very interested. I had to answer this in a way that gave them hope.

"Some of them, yes. Others, less so. I grew up in the human world, not even knowing what I was. It has given me human friends and a human life. From what I know of the humans I interacted with, there are a mix of maturity and levels of empathy and understanding. If it was done in the right way and with the right representatives, I think it could work."

By the time I finished speaking, I had the attention of all the elders and they were looking at me as if I might be some kind of god. I didn't know what part of what I'd said had done it, but I'd clearly given them the answer they wanted to hear.

It made me uncomfortable, but if they thought I could give them what they wanted, it might help secure their assistance. After all, this was politics. They had something I wanted—dragons who would brave danger and lend me their magic—and I had something they wanted as queen—the ability to decide whether to finally reveal us to the world.

With this knowledge, I relaxed a little. I thought I

understood this diplomacy game better, but I wasn't about to make an offer to the city without having talked to my friends and the dragons I trusted first. For now, that was as far as our conversation could go, and that helped me relax and enjoy the meal.

Letting the dragons around me carry more of the conversation, I listened to them talk about anything and everything and finished eating.

It wasn't long before the subject of Detaris came up. It caught my attention, and I guessed I would be dragged into the conversation once more.

"We communicate with the elders in Detaris fairly frequently, and of course, technology has made that easier lately, so human progress hasn't all been bad." Valkin smiled, but his gaze fixed on me. "They said something confusing recently that perhaps you could clear up."

"I can certainly try." A knot formed in my stomach. This felt like a crunch point, where I could easily lose their respect or desire to cooperate, no matter what else they wanted. It might be beyond my control. I had no idea what Detaris might have said.

"A few weeks ago they said that they were crowning you and you would be the new queen and had proved that you were the heir to their satisfaction. Yet a few days later, maybe a week, they informed us that you had withdrawn your claim to the throne and that they would not recommend that any of us recognized you as the heir to the throne. When your friends approached us and told us that you were the next legitimate queen, we grew even more confused."

"I can understand that," I replied, trying to buy some

time to properly structure my response. "It's been confusing to live through it as the possible heir as well. I hope that I can make this a little simpler on all of you. I was left with little choice in Detaris but to withdraw my claim. For a reason I cannot explain or comprehend fully, the city doesn't like red dragons much, and they were never particularly accepting of me. When I found out who my mother and father were, and that the gate was in danger as well, I assumed that I needed to become the next big leader to unite our race and have them all attend a ritual to recharge it."

"And they didn't like this?" the elderly woman across from me asked.

"Not exactly. Many in Detaris have, or had, decided that the gate was fine, and despite me showing them evidence to the contrary, they don't think they need a red dragon at all, let alone one who thinks they ought to be a queen."

"It sounds as if you have quite a story to tell."

"Not one that I enjoy telling. I had thought Detaris was my home and instead I have found that they don't want anything to do with me and have rejected the people I care about as well as endangered us all by refusing to acknowledge that the gate is in urgent need of repair and a magical recharge. One of the elders offered to travel to the gate and document its state, and bring all the findings back to Detaris, but they even exiled him. He's here, in this room, today with us."

Several of the elders rubbernecked around to Liam, who in turn was looking at Griffin. Perhaps they'd continue their probing into Detaris' strange behavior later, after dinner, and leave me out of it. I had considered being careful with what I said in case the elders in this city had strong bonds with those in Detaris, but I couldn't lie and continue to respect myself.

Mostly, I had been as surprised by the reaction of Detaris as anyone else, and I hoped I'd managed to convey that if nothing else.

CHAPTER FIVE

When I woke up it took me a moment to recognize where I was. It was my bedroom in Trellian and my fourth day here.

Since arriving and the first dinner with the elders, I hadn't done much that could have been considered political. We chilled out, saw more of the city, and talked to different dragons. I'd also scanned for shadow catchers each day, wanting to check if they felt me and if so, what they were doing.

The first day or two there had been so little shadow catcher activity that I hadn't worried about it, but now that we'd been here a little longer, I felt more of them gathering nearby and coming to the shores of the lake. It was as if they were trying to work out where I was and felt me but hadn't realized that I was on the water.

It didn't bode well for us traveling to Isethnore, and I was already trying to think of how I could break it to Hiachi that we might not be able to—at least not yet. As it was, I was thinking that if we didn't leave here soon, it would be too difficult. And that meant that it was time to wrap everything up and get to some agreement.

For that, I needed to pull together the dragons I wanted advice from and work out what I could offer in exchange for support from this city. More than once, they had brought up their troubles about getting supplies in a modern human world that made it so hard to hide, made worse by the lack of land nearby and the more suspicious human population around them. They were struggling and they wanted to know I cared.

I understood them, but it's easy to promise something without being sure you can deliver and then disappoint people later. That wasn't something I wanted to do either.

Before my thoughts overwhelmed me, I got up and padded to the dining area to eat breakfast. Alitas was already up, another honor guard with him, and my mother, Reijo, and Ben were there.

Neritas and Flick must be sleeping, along with everyone else, but I knew they wouldn't be long if I started talking. The pair had taken to sleeping with their door ajar, and when they heard my voice and knew I was up, they quickly emerged to see what was going on.

My mother pushed a plate toward me and offered me some breakfast. "You're up early."

"I can feel the demons coming closer and gathering. They've worked out that I'm here."

"You'd think they'd have realized they can't win against you by now and run away instead," Reijo replied.

"When you're in service to the devil and he doesn't give up, there's not much you can do but keep throwing yourself at the enemy," Ben pointed out, looking through the journal open in front of him. It wasn't one I recognized. He'd spent the last few days searching the library here to see if anything there could help us.

He made a good point, but it wouldn't help me today. The demons were coming and I had to figure out what to do in response.

"I'm thinking of going before the elders today and making a proposal. Get them to ask their city for volunteers and offer something in return." I got everyone's attention as I spoke, and Ben finally looked up from the book.

Alitas was the first to respond, my honor guard the most experienced in politics. "If you're only asking them to gather volunteers, you should be careful what you promise. No matter how much they might agree with our ideals, they might not wish to get involved in this fight."

"That's what I wanted to talk to all of you about," I said as I saw Neritas appear from his room and caught a brief glimpse through the open door of Flick pulling on a shirt.

I spent the next few minutes telling my group what I thought I had picked up on and what I believed the dragons in this city were hoping I would do for them.

Reijo, my mom, and Alitas asked me the most questions, getting me to explain why I thought what I did. I ate while we talked and they considered the best course of action.

"From the few conversations I have had with the dragons in the city, I think you're right," Ben said. "They seem to want to stop hiding and pretending, although they're not eager to integrate with humanity just yet. They don't want to struggle."

"I think we can all understand that," I replied. "But I need to make sure I offer them something in my power. I don't know if it's wise to let humanity know about us. I don't think there's another way to solve their problems, however."

"It's something I've been thinking about since I got here." Reijo leaned forward. "I still have a lot of financial resources and, as you're aware, the ability to help in that regard, but even with having more money, it doesn't solve the difficulty of getting the supplies here undetected. The ships are noticed now."

Reijo's words confirmed what I feared. The only solution for this city was to relocate or reveal themselves to at least a few people. And the former wasn't feasible or practical. No, I had to talk to them about letting humanity know about us.

Flick also joined us, his hair freshly gelled in place, and I welcomed the extra opinion to the debate as we discussed the controversial topic of humanity and what they were likely to do in reaction to finding out that magic and dragons existed and always had.

We were still talking about it when the rest of our group appeared and the local dragons arrived, along with Valkin, to see how we were that morning and if we needed anything.

"It seems we have interrupted you all in a very important conversation," the elder said, although he did not indicate that he had heard any particulars. "Would you like us to leave you to it?"

"No." I stood. "We might be animated, but I think we're mostly in agreement and the details can wait. Thank you for offering us the space, but I actually think I'd like to have an audience with the elders of the city if that's agreeable to all of you. I have much to say and I'd like to hear your views on several things as well."

"We would welcome such an event. Let me go back to the elders and gather them. Would half an hour be too delayed?"

"Half an hour would be swift. Please don't rush. There is no disastrous event that will occur in the meantime. Please, simply let the other elders know and give them the time they would need at their own pace. I can be summoned when you are ready for me."

"That is most gracious of you, Princess. Our old bones can be weary and hard to move at any great pace sometimes. We'll endeavor not to keep you waiting too long, however."

I bowed to the elder as he did the same to me, surprising him with politeness. I knew it was earning me good favor. It made a difference to treat people with respect and dignity and not to act as if I was above them. I wasn't. I still was just an LA orphan in a lot of ways.

Within an hour I was summoned to the elders' chamber. I took several honor guards, Reijo, my mother, Jace, Neritas, and Flick with me. Ben declined the invitation to accompany me, not wanting our party to overwhelm with numbers and knowing that he couldn't offer much with his limited knowledge and lack of practical offerings, such as Reijo's fund or my mother's insight into the red-dragon skills.

The Trellian elders' chamber wasn't too different from the one in Detaris, and I quickly found the lie-detecting device that sat underneath the floor in the center. I connected to it before I noticed that no one else in the room was doing so.

I waited and watched as I thanked them for coming together for us and listened as they made a little polite small talk. Unlike the times when I went before the elders in Detaris, these dragons offered us chairs and made us a lot more comfortable.

Appreciating the more trusting and less formal atmosphere, I relaxed a little.

"Thank you for letting me come before you and for giving me such a warm welcome in your city. I can truly say that I have enjoyed my time here and felt as if it is a home away from home."

"You're very welcome to stay here for as long as you wish," Valkin replied. I nodded my thanks, catching the truth in the words and feeling grateful for them. I was liked if nothing else, and that would make my task easier.

"I appreciate you making such a kind offer, but I fear that I cannot take you all up on it. At least not during the current state of affairs. While I have been here, the demons have slowly all made their way closer. I have already explained that many of them are still hunting me wherever I go. If I stay much longer before they are dealt with for good, I will endanger you all too much. As much as I would love to stay longer, I must move on and take the danger with me."

"This is unwelcome news, as it must be tiresome and frustrating for you to feel chased from place to place," the eldest of the dragons offered. Her high-pitched voice was gentle.

"It definitely has its downsides, but that is why I am before you all now. I believe that if we can strengthen the gate, we stand a good chance of being able to diminish the numbers of these foul creatures and make the whole world safer. I've come before you today to make a request, but to also offer my services as much as I can in return."

"Then we will hear and consider both with the good intentions they are made from and hope that we can all go away from this with easier minds." Valkin smiled, and everyone else murmured in agreement. So far so good.

I made my request quickly, mentioning the danger to anyone joining me, but also the benefit. I stayed truthful but made it clear that I needed volunteers.

"I will aid you, with what skill I have," one of the young guards jumped in before his elders could respond. "I don't believe I am as strong as some of your honor guards, but I am eager to do the duty of protecting those who need it."

"Then you can do so, Selgar." Valkin nodded toward the dragon. "And we will offer the opportunity to the rest of the city, but please, Princess, continue and forgive the interruption."

"There is nothing to forgive," I replied as I gathered my thoughts and tried to think of where I was. "Thank you for agreeing to my request without hearing my offer. I will make it gladly anyway. It is clear that your city is struggling with supplies, finances, and the seemingly endless expansion of humanity. While I don't know of the exact solution that is best right in this moment, I give you my word I will do what I can to aid you."

"Do you have any ideas?" one of the quieter elders

spoke up, his voice stronger than I'd have expected from his thin frame.

"I think there's a good chance that it will have to involve humans and let at least some of them know about this city. How many, which ones, and where is still a matter to be determined and something I would work very closely with your city on. It is all very well my companions and me debating what we think is best, but it impacts all of you far more and you should get to have a significant say in how the current difficulties are dealt with."

"And do you have a timeline for when you hope to help us?" Valkin asked. His voice sounded more suspicious and did nothing to ease my fears.

"Not exactly, but it would be a big priority once the gate is more secure. It will do nothing to aid any of us if the demon behind it gets free. Making our whole race safe has to be my top priority. I also think that humanity is naturally finding us here and there and they have noticed on several occasions that I am active in a way they don't understand. Continuing to fight the demons is only going to bring even more attention to our kind. There is a good chance that solving one problem will present a solution to the other."

It was clear from the device in the floor that this response surprised them, but it also eased the tension. For me to admit that either way humanity was likely to discover us all soon wasn't something they'd expected, but it was a good point in response.

"Thank you," Valkin said a few seconds later, almost as if he wasn't sure what to say either. I felt a tinge of disappointment in the room. It wasn't as much of a promise as they'd hoped for. I knew that, but I couldn't help but think of the warning my friends had given me earlier to not promise too much.

Before I could try to reassure them or accept that this was the best I could do, there was a knock at the door and an aide I'd seen on the previous day came rushing in with one of the dragon tablets in his hands. Not looking at me, but with a pale face and hurried feet, he approached Valkin and leaned in to talk.

Within seconds Valkin took the tablet and read something on it, his eyes growing wider as he did.

"Forgive me." He looked up and around the room before looking directly at me. "Am I correct in thinking that you've not heard the latest news from Detaris?"

I shook my head, feeling my stomach sink as he spoke. Whatever this was going to be, I got the feeling it wasn't going to be good.

"They have declared that another heir to the throne has come forward and they have recognized his legitimacy. He will be crowned in just two days."

Swallowing, I couldn't process what I'd just heard. The words echoed around in my head. How could it be possible?

How could they have found another red dragon so suddenly?

CHAPTER SIX

The silence slowly faded as the elders all sought to read the message just delivered to them. My mother stepped forward to do the same for us and it soon became clear that the elders had spoken the truth. Someone in Detaris had discovered a new red dragon and they'd come to claim the throne.

"I obviously know as little of this situation as you do," my mother said, addressing the room as I had done. "But I hope that I can add some extra information to the matter that you don't have currently. As you know, I am the widow of your previous king. When he died, he knew that there were so few red dragons left that he needed to protect our daughter to ensure that the strongest line to the throne remained intact."

"Are you suggesting that this is an impostor?" Valkin asked.

"Not necessarily an impostor. Scarlet does have some relations, and there were other family lines that could have produced a distant heir. It's possible that this red dragon is in the royal line. But I am certain they won't have as strong a claim to the throne as Scarlet does."

"As she's the daughter of the last monarch, I'm not sure anyone could have a stronger claim than her," Alitas added.

"We've been asked to recognize them as our monarch and to make the usual pledge to serve them." Valkin sounded pained as he said this, as if he knew this would cause trouble and was worried that we might not like it.

"You should do what you think is best for your city." I stepped forward, my legs threatening not to hold me up any longer. "In light of this information, I will need to consult with my companions and discuss how this impacts us."

I wanted to add so much more, but nothing else would come out, my mind getting in the way as I realized that this would change so many things, including everything I could do and offer.

No one stopped me as I walked out of the room and headed toward our suite. Neritas, Flick, and Alitas were the first to follow, rushing to catch up.

By the time I reached the guest building and plonked myself down on a dining chair, everyone had caught up. They sat themselves down around me, no one speaking for some time.

"This changes everything," I said to no one in particular.

"It does. And it's something I don't want to say, but I'm going to have to go to Detaris." Alitas studied my face, sadness in his eyes.

"Because you serve the monarch." I didn't need him to explain why. It was obvious now he'd said it.

"I don't want to leave you unprotected. Never before in

my time in the honor guard have I felt divided. But I do now."

"I'm not being an honor guard for anyone else," Neritas said. "I only agreed to protect you. You're my queen."

Although this wasn't a new statement from Neritas, he said it with a conviction that made tears prick at my eyes and a lump form in my throat. I didn't feel like a queen. I felt as if I was a failure.

"We might need to take this back a step." Ben shuffled closer. "This red dragon they say they have could be an impostor, could be someone we thought was dead, could be a fake and not even be a red dragon, or might not even exist. There are so many unknowns."

"I think I'd like to have a plan for what to do in some of the more likely situations," I replied, smiling and taking his hand briefly to show that I appreciated him trying to calm us down.

This was going to be difficult to work through and think of all the outcomes, and we were in desperate need of more information before making decisions, but we were only going to get more information from one place. I didn't want to go to Detaris without a backup plan or two for whatever we found.

"Let's assume that they have a legitimate heir. That no one is lying, no one has come back from the dead and he's another red dragon with a decent claim. It doesn't matter if they're a distant cousin and I had the stronger claim to the throne. I officially renounced my claim. He would have every right to be accepted, wouldn't he?" I looked at Alitas as I finished speaking, knowing he would have the answer.

"Technically yes, but you are able to change your mind before the coronation."

"And if I did change my mind, they'd have to crown me instead?"

"I think you'd have the support of this city if nothing else," Reijo added, sitting forward.

"So, if I want to stop this other dragon I have to get to Detaris before he's crowned?"

"Yes." Alitas didn't take his eyes off me, curiosity in his expression.

"Please tell us that's what you want to do." Neritas took my other hand. "Please tell us you'll stop all this madness."

I didn't reply right away, thinking about the question. Did I want to take the throne simply to stop someone else from taking it? The notion of doing so was tempting, but I couldn't bring myself to do it, and it would only divide the dragon community further if the citizens of Detaris were willing to crown this new dragon.

Could I be responsible for causing even more of a divide?

"I don't know," I finally replied. "It would depend on what this other dragon is like and how much support they have."

"There aren't many possibilities of who it could be," my mom said. She suggested a few, all dragons who came from weak lines.

"None of these dragons sound like they could boil an egg with their powers, let alone fry a demon." Flick pulled a face that he reserved for when he was the most unimpressed. I grinned, grateful for the humor in his words and the roundabout way of showing me support.

"No matter how strong they are, the honor guard will need to go serve them if they're crowned." Alitas exhaled and looked down at his hands. He shook his head a couple of times before turning his gaze back to me. "I wouldn't normally ask anyone to do anything they didn't want to, but, Red, it would make this a lot simpler if you stopped worrying about the idiots in Detaris and demanded the throne anyway. I can stand with you as the rightful heir."

"I won't make any promises. I don't want to be a queen. The gate is my priority."

"You know that's why we all want to serve you, right?" Neritas hadn't given up. "You aren't trying to be anyone important, just do the job you feel you have to."

As another silence fell, I looked around the room. None of them had given up on the idea of me being queen, but there was a good chance I would let them down.

It made me anxious to think of Alitas taking the honor guards to protect someone else and leaving me to tackle the gate alone. More than a few times, they had saved my life, and in declaring that I was an heir I had painted a target on my back. I hadn't been living in Detaris recently, but there were other dragons who could take issue with me.

With everyone in Trellian having met me and appearing to like me, and Hiachi from Isethnore I was sure I would get more support, but it was a big risk.

"I haven't said anything yet, Red," Jace interrupted my thoughts. "But I'm going to before you get too deep into whatever thought is running through your head. We're not supporting anyone else. We've been kicked out of Detaris anyway and I want that gate taken care of. Unless this dragon is three times more powerful than you, hot, and willing to work with all of us too, I'm not even going to meet the guy."

I smiled at her description of the possible reasons she'd accept an alternative over me, but it was little help to me when I was trying to work out what to do. If Alitas had to go to Detaris, it barely mattered what the rest of us did. Our journey here had been to collect new dragons and boost the power we had to tackle the gate.

If we lost the entire honor guard, we would lose far more than we could gain from five similar cities. I had to decide what to do for the best, but all I could think about was how little I knew.

"There's nothing else for it. We're all going to have to go back to Detaris and find out who this is and what they intend to do about the gate."

"Nothing, if Brenta gets her way," Jace pointed out.

I tried not to think about it and hoped enough people in the city understood that it wouldn't be any harder. Several of the city guards who had seen the gate had been allowed to stay in Detaris. They had understood the peril.

"Detaris it is, even if most of us end up banished." Ben grinned as if this was the funniest thing anyone had said in weeks, and Neritas joined him.

I shook my head as everyone got up and returned to their rooms to pack. With my rucksack still full of everything that mattered, I had very little packing to do.

When it came to the city and the conversation with the elders that had been interrupted, I knew I would have to go back to them and try to explain. I could only hope that Hiachi understood why I wouldn't yet be able to go onward to his city as we had planned. We'd gotten along well so far, I knew it was partially because he expected I had something to offer them.

If I wasn't queen, I couldn't offer them anything. Their support wasn't guaranteed.

Wanting to go back to the elders, I took a purposeful stride toward the door and the bridge that connected my building to the next. The dragon assigned to aid us appeared from a nearby house and came over to me.

"Is there anything I can get you?" she asked, smiling as if she didn't know the news.

Sure she didn't and not trusting my voice yet, I shook my head.

My mother came up from behind me. "Thank you for all the help you've given us. We're going to have to go sooner than we planned and need to talk more to the elders about it. I hope we can sort everything out soon and return to your wonderful city."

The aide nodded and her mouth slipped open. Hesitation filled me as I considered how rudely I might have come across, but I carried on past her and went back to the elders' chamber.

All of the elders were still there, talking over the same news. They stopped when they saw me in the doorway and once more I hesitated.

"I'm sorry to intrude again, but I thought you would appreciate knowing our plans now that we have new ones.

"Yes, Princess. Please come inside. We have further thoughts as well and are interested in hearing your own now we've all had time to compose ourselves."

"Firstly, thank you for all you have done to host us and

make us comfortable here. We appreciate the welcome and we're sorry to have to go sooner than we planned. It seems important that we return to Detaris, and not only meet the red dragon who has come forward, but also discuss with the elders there what this means for many of us. I hope this isn't going to create too many difficulties for you and your plans."

As I looked around at the elders I saw the same uncertainty. This was alarming to them as well, and they didn't know what to do.

"We hope you can return to us soon. In different times, there is much we would like to discuss with you and improve together."

"Then I will return as soon as I can to continue our discussion."

"Do you plan to leave for Detaris immediately?" one of the women asked as I stepped away.

I stopped and studied her. "As soon as possible. Why do you ask?"

"Several of our citizens wish to go there as well, including myself. I know I would feel better about their safety if they were to travel with a larger group, especially one with experience in the human world."

"Then consider them and yourself welcome to travel with us as long as they can be ready to leave within two hours. I cannot wait any longer than that." I hoped that was a reasonable amount of time. I was swift to pack and so were most of my usual companions, but the dragons from this city were unlikely to have traveled before.

"They will be ready when you leave. You have my thanks. And once again, our apologies that this visit has not gone in the direction any of us would have liked it to. In different circumstances, I am sure we could have helped each other greatly."

As the dragons bowed at me, my brain whirred. I bowed back as I thought through all the possible meanings her words could have and came to only one conclusion. They had been about to accept me as their queen and offer me their full support.

"I still hope that this can be resolved in a manner that suits us all," I replied.

It didn't promise them anything specific, but it did make it clear that I wasn't giving up. Until I knew more about this other red dragon, I couldn't give up. If my mother was right, they didn't have a very good claim to the throne. But did I want it? Could I take it?

CHAPTER SEVEN

The party with me on the way to Detaris was a strange bunch, and it had grown yet again. I was looking over the group as we took up several tables in a fast-food restaurant when my mother leaned in closer to me.

"You might not feel as if you're uniting anyone, but you have more people with you and learning from you than ever. These dragons might not be a perfect bunch or have chosen to sit beside each other in the human world on their own, but they all have something in common."

"What's that?" I asked. On some subconscious level, I knew, but I wanted to hear my mother's thoughts on the group.

"They recognize your authority and natural skill as a leader. You were born to lead them."

I frowned. It wasn't something I wanted to claim, even with my reaction to learning another was in the line to the throne. I didn't want the throne so much as to stop someone else who was unfit from taking it.

I'd already decided that if we got to Detaris and this guy

was capable and would take the threat of the demon seriously, I would happily step aside. It would make my life so much easier if he would handle it all. But I hadn't said a word to anyone.

"You'll never be entirely comfortable being a leader," Mom added. "Which is exactly why you will make a good one. You question yourself and let others give you counsel, yet you strive to make things happen that you think will be best for everyone. It's a combination that a lot of red dragons before you lacked."

"Yet a lot of them still hate me," I replied. We'd been through a lot of this before, but here we were again.

"They don't hate you. They fear a whole heap of different things and think you represent some of those fears. Fear makes people do things they're not proud of."

If nothing else she'd said to me in this conversation was true, that one very much was. Fear twisted people and their intentions, and it made them do things they wouldn't have done if they were rational.

Either way, I would lead this little group and hope I could carry on. I got the feeling that even if this other dragon was respectable, several of my crew would never let me persuade them that I wasn't a queen. As we got closer to Detaris, I grew more and more nervous that they would act unpredictably.

Neritas had already changed the course of my life once by declaring me the heir before I was ready, giving me little choice but to go along with it as if that had been my plan all along. I didn't want something like that to happen again.

I didn't get much more of a chance to think about it. We finished up and got back on the road, and I was once again sandwiched in a car with the four people who stuck by my side the most when we weren't in a safe place. Neritas was brooding and silent, but Flick handled his nerves by talking even more.

We were only a few hours from Detaris, and the miles flew by as Ben drove and Flick talked. Alitas kept glancing at me as if he had something on his mind but didn't want to interrupt my friend, and I tried to not let any of what I was feeling show. It was a strange end to the journey but it was soon over.

Ben led our convoy and drove us right up to the barrier. As he was driving off the road, I noticed a tent on the opposite side of the road with several people sitting in camping chairs. They leaped to their feet when they saw Ben take the direction he did.

My body went cold. "I think they were humans trying to figure out the entrance."

"Not our problem if we're not welcome in Detaris," Neritas spoke for the first time since we'd left, and the anger in his voice took me by surprise.

Although he had a point, it wouldn't help our case if the elders in Detaris were angry at us for showing humans where the hidden road to the city was.

None of us had seen them in time, however, and our convoy was all through the barrier and stopping on the road ahead of the small parking lot before I could suggest that a few of the cars didn't follow.

Neritas and Flick were quick to get out, but I paused, not sure I wanted to face whatever came next. I would be scrutinized and judged again, and it wasn't pleasant.

After a few seconds, Neritas leaned down to check on

me and offer me his hand. Grateful, I took it and let him help me from the car. I hadn't accepted the gesture because I needed aid in exiting the vehicle gracefully, but because I wanted moral support from someone who believed in me beyond a shadow of a doubt.

Dragons reacted to our presence very quickly, no doubt recognizing the vehicles we were using. Capricia came swooping in, transforming from the white dragon in the sky to a human as she touched down on land. Several dragons that I recognized in both forms came with her, the city guards, and several elders. The elders stayed behind the guards.

I saw what I'd come for: the red gleam of the guy claiming the throne I was meant to have.

He flew in but far slower than the others and landed farther back. When he transformed I lost sight of him for a moment. Too many others were crowding in.

With my entire group looking at me, I had no choice but to be the one to approach them. Even Alitas and the diplomats waited for me to make the first move.

The usual group who stuck close to me fell in behind as I walked toward Brenta and Capricia.

"I believe we told you that you were exiled from Detaris," Capricia said, the dislike clear in her voice.

"You did, but I'm a red dragon in line to the throne. Whether I claim it or not, I'm still going where I like. Feel free to try and stop me, but I think we both know who would win if you did." I wasn't sure where my confidence had come from, but she snapped her mouth shut and glared at me.

To give her pride a little relief I turned my attention to Brenta.

"We were in Trellian when we heard that another red dragon had come forward to try and claim the throne. I want to meet him, and so do representatives of Trellian." I spoke before Brenta could, and her eyes narrowed as she glanced beyond and then focused on me again.

"That is up to him." She held my gaze, her expression haughtier than it had been previously.

The temptation to connect to their magic and suck the power out of them rose inside me and took me by surprise. In good conscience, I couldn't do something like that, and I wasn't going to, but it was possible. I got the feeling that I could have fought most of the city with what I knew now and all the practice I'd had fighting shadow catchers near the gate.

"If someone is going to try and tell the dragon world they have a better claim to the throne than I do, I think he had better meet me and say it to my face, don't you?"

A tense silence settled in response to my words.

"You renounced your claim," Capricia said a few seconds later.

"Only because I believed that Detaris didn't want a monarch and that they spoke for the rest of the dragon population. Since I've now found that neither is true, it changes a lot, don't you think?"

None of them could deny it. They were my reasons, and the whole of Detaris knew it.

Before I could say anything else, Griffin came forward.

"Brenta, Detaris has always served the red-dragon line

and the other cities. You have to consider that crowning a different dragon may not be the right course."

"I don't have to do anything that you ask of me. You are also exiled and in disgrace."

"For supporting me when you didn't want to. Get over yourself, Brenta," I lashed out. My temper rose and I couldn't help it. The words had tumbled out before I could stop myself.

Brenta looked like I'd slapped her and I took the moment it gave me to think.

I took a step back and scanned the dragons hovering or resting on the edges of the city and the number who had taken human form to get closer. Somewhere in this crowd, their future king was hiding.

"I know you can hear me, red dragon. Are you afraid of me? Or will you talk to me and give us a chance to resolve this in a way that is satisfactory to both of us?"

I paused as murmurs of conversation rippled outward from where I stood. The challenge was subtle, but it was a challenge nonetheless. If this dragon was going to show he could be king, he needed to respond to me.

Brenta opened her mouth, but before she could speak, the crowd shifted and someone came forward.

"You're not in charge here," he said as he stepped out.

"Neither are you," I replied, studying him.

He was about my height, his hair darker, almost brown, red, and he was skinny. He was also younger than me, at a guess. He looked as if he was trying to grow a beard, but he wasn't succeeding, and instead of the flaming red I'd have expected from a dragon of our color, it was, like his hair, more brown than red.

I reached out tentatively with my magic to feel for his and see if I could gauge his skill or strength. I connected to him easily enough from such a short distance but didn't feel much strength. His eyes widened a little as if he'd felt me, but I made sure not to pull any energy from him. Although I'd never tried to measure the strength of a dragon this way before, he didn't feel as if he had much power or any idea of what to do with it.

I wasn't impressed.

"This discussion shouldn't take place out in the open," one of the other elders said. "And there are other matters of concern."

"Yes, there are, like the humans you have watching your entrance and exit from the city. I think they're trying to work out where you are and how to get in," I said, throwing caution to the wind.

"We should have a meeting on neutral ground," Capricia said and moved to the red dragon's side. I saw the glance he gave her and the hint of uncertainty in his eyes, but it vanished as swiftly as it had appeared, leaving me to wonder if I had imagined it.

For a red dragon who was meant to be taking the throne, he wasn't as impressive as I'd expected him to be. Was he more of a puppet than anything else?

"There's a diner not far from here that knows our kind and has kept our secrets for years. We could talk there." Ben stepped forward, reminding everyone that he was one of the more experienced dragons when it came to the outside world. He had been a respected and powerful member of the dragon community as well.

More than once he had given a command and other

dragons had given way to his expertise and knowledge. They did this time as well. Brenta nodded and accepted his suggestion for the would-be king.

This was yet another indicator that he wasn't an entirely free agent. Capricia continued to glare at me as she was commanded to get sufficient guards ready to protect him. She flicked her gaze to Alitas, and I noted that he hadn't offered to serve anyone but me yet. I considered leaving some of my group here, especially the diplomats and the members of Jace's organization who were mostly with us to fight shadow catchers, but there could be a benefit to them witnessing how Detaris treated me and the differences between me and Brenta, Capricia, and their heir.

It helped that I had Alitas standing beside me still, his loyalty to me clear as we moved toward the cars again. We walked toward our car, and the crowd parted just enough to allow us through.

Ben sat in the driver's seat waiting for the dragons in Detaris to prepare themselves. A horde of guards joined the convoy to protect the elders and the new dragon—another five cars, which made us an almost even group. Of course, the dragons in my crew were generally stronger and of more varied colors. If I battled a dragon, I would have the advantage unless he was skilled enough to connect to my guard and take their magic. I doubted he was capable of that.

I also knew that a lot of my magic skills and my understanding of them had changed when I communed with the ancestors on Kilnar. I was sure this dragon hadn't been there to do the same. It wouldn't surprise me to find that he didn't know it existed.

Finally, our group set off, heading back out of the city and startling the humans waiting on the other side. It was obvious where the entrance was, and I noticed that two of them had phones out and were recording everything.

Amused and aware that, as an exiled dragon, I had no specific rules to obey, I waved. If they wanted proof that something crazy was happening here, I didn't mind giving them a little more.

"Be careful, Red. They'll have the cars tracked and we could find law enforcement joining us." Ben glanced at me through the rearview mirror.

"If they wanted to arrest us they would have probably done it already. I doubt anyone in any sort of authority wants to take the chance that these videos aren't elaborate hoaxes." It was something we had thought about and discussed. There were several social media reports of our kind now, and I was front and center in several videos.

"We'll keep this meeting as short as we can." Alitas also gave me a look. The kind that was halfway between a plea and a stern expression warning me to listen to him. It took all my self-control not to laugh or smile at it.

"I doubt it will take more than five minutes for Scarlet to show this guy that she's in charge and he needs to back down. He didn't look like he could stand up to Neritas, let alone Red when she's in fight mode." Flick grinned as he patted my leg. I glared at him, as much for the physical contact as the deliberately patronizing smirk he had.

"I'm sure Red will make him wish he was any color but," Neritas replied, joining in.

"Be careful what you assume. I've seen dragons who look like nothing in human form and fool everyone around them into thinking they are harmless and then toppled whole cities." Alitas broke through the humor in an instant, the seriousness of his words and the look on his face enough to make everyone stop and think.

The car journey was almost entirely silent and tense. I didn't know what to say to my companions after Alitas had reprimanded us for not taking the threat seriously. He had a good point and we shouldn't go into this lightly. Neritas and Flick felt the weight of that now as well.

I had a lot of questions running through my head. What if this happened? What if he was powerful? What if he did know what he was doing? What if he tried to kill me? What if I was forced to kill him to save the world or something like that?

A lot of the worrying was unnecessary. I would have my answers as soon as we reached the diner and I could have a proper conversation with this dragon. All I had to do was keep my cool and find out what I could.

CHAPTER EIGHT

We weren't far away when I recognized the diner. It was one Ben had brought me to in the past once. When looking for Anthony and not sure where we could go, we had brought lobsters here and exchanged them for a hearty meal. The chef had appeared to have a sweet spot for Ben and I was curious if that had continued or if she was the same way with other dragons of power.

Nine cars and a van, each carrying at least four people, all pulling up to the same diner was enough to attract a lot of attention from everyone already there, but it was a quiet weekday afternoon, and most of the patrons seemed to be regulars just going about their lives.

The waitress stared at us as we all got out and naturally divided into two groups. Ben and I led the way with Alitas, Jace, Griffin, Neritas, and Flick close behind. Almost my entire group was inside before Capricia and the city guard followed. The waitress looked at me and Ben and then past us, shifting her body weight as she leaned to the side to look down at the group.

"Are you all wanting to eat in?" she asked.

"I think so," Ben replied. "Let Alice know her good friend Benjamin is here and he brought along a few friends who need some extra care. At least two of them are the special color. She'll understand what that means."

The waitress nodded, clearly relieved to be getting an instruction that let her off the hook of deciding what to do with us. If her boss knew about us, then we were her boss' problem. We spread out along the bar, keeping out of the way of the regulars as more and more dragons came inside. Some of the latter group—the guards mostly—waited outside, since there wasn't enough space inside.

We didn't have to wait long. The waitress soon reappeared, and the chef bustled out after her. The chef was the woman who had served us, cooked for us, and handled our check the first time we were here, but she looked a little less pleased to see us than she had the last time. Her eyes eventually settled on Ben, but they flicked to me and took in my red hair.

"Okay, I won't deny you've been a good customer over the years, Benjamin, but there's got to be at least forty in your party and you've given me no warning. I can seat you all, but—"

Ben lifted his hand and cut off her words.

"You don't need to fret. We didn't have a plan we could have warned you of, or I swear I would have, but we're also happy with whatever you can manage."

"We could do with some privacy, however." Griffin stepped forward and spoke in a way that was brave for him. "We would appreciate it if you could help us with that."

This made her frown deepen, but she looked at the group of us and then at the four regulars scattered around the bar. One of them immediately downed the last of a cup of coffee and pulled a bill out of his pocket. As he slapped it down on the counter, he gave Ben and Griffin a nod.

"I'll help make the decision a little easier and head off for the day. Feed 'em up and let them have the place. The rest of us can be happy you're getting the business."

This had a better impact than anything we had said. If her regulars weren't going to mind and we had money to burn, it made sense for her to accommodate us.

"Okay. What kind of seating arrangement do you need? I can't put you all together. There's just no way to do it in this fixed arrangement."

"It's okay. A lot of the group are guards who can simply sit or stand around us in groups." Griffin smiled and moved closer to the chef. It was as if the elder had stepped into his element, and between the two of them and some willing extras to act as muscles and take directions, they rearranged the interior of the diner. The waitress took care of the three other regulars, finishing up their service and encouraging them to pay and head home.

It was more efficient than I'd expected, and for a few minutes, I felt as if I was a loose end. I wasn't encouraged to help move the tables, and the tension between the two groups of dragons was clear to everyone. All of us were hoping to get on with the discussion we were there to have.

My mother helped to rescue things. Pulling out some paper and a pen, she started to take drinks orders from everyone. The guards positioned themselves in booths around the diner, and Alitas and the diplomats from Trellian encouraged me to join them off to one side to peruse a menu. For a moment all the animosity was forgotten as we focused on the basic need for sustenance.

By the time the tables were rearranged and everyone was directed to seats, Mom had done half the work for our hosts, and what we had ordered so far was looked at gratefully.

"Well, if nothing else, you're all organized and helpful about this. I appreciate it," the chef said as she came over to me and Mom.

"Least we could do when you're being so accommodating," I replied. "I just hope we don't run you out of anything."

"I keep the place well stocked, but we'll see. I have local suppliers and make a lot myself, so it just means more work for me tomorrow to replenish, but I can spread the wealth a little too. Not something any of us will complain about."

This put a smile on all our faces and made it clear why Ben had suggested we come here. She had been shocked, but she had a good attitude and was willing to work hard to accommodate her customers, whoever they might be. I hoped that we could make it worth her while financially to have us all in there.

Finally, we were all sitting down, with food and drinks ordered, and the waitress and chef were busy doing their respective jobs. They had turned the sign to Closed so no one else would come in and disturb us. I felt a little guilty when the waitress had to turn a young couple away partway through serving our drinks, but they didn't seem too bothered and promised to come back later.

With lots to discuss, as soon as everyone had a drink and the waitress had gone to help the chef in the kitchen, we all looked at each other. I was sitting in the middle of a long table with my group of dragons on one side and our counterparts opposite us. With only Griffin representing the elders on my side, the diplomats from Trellian were also treated like part of my delegation.

It worked, and it gave me another chance to study the red dragon I'd only just met.

"I'm Scarlet," I said to open the conversation.

"Grigick," he replied.

As he said his name I detected a slight accent, but I couldn't place it. I got the impression that he didn't want it to show.

"Well, Grigick, I must admit, it's nice to know that I'm not the only red dragon left alive." I figured it was worth starting with something positive. I didn't know if I liked this guy or not, but knowing he existed gave me hope that more red dragons existed out there.

"I'm sure there's not just the two of us in the whole world. There are many cities and many dragons, and not all of them like to communicate much."

It was an interesting response, and it hinted at how much more knowledge he had of the world we were in than I did.

"Sometimes I wonder, but you're probably right, Grigick. Which city did you grow up in?"

"I have lived in many of them across the world. My father moved me around a lot. He was...a restless soul."

I lifted my eyebrows at this description, noticing the pause and wondering if he was covering for something else. Our eyes met briefly and he quickly looked down and away, focusing on his drink.

"It must have been both wonderful to see so much of the world and difficult to keep leaving your home behind and starting somewhere new." I could relate to this very well. I'd lived in a lot of different homes and never felt settled anywhere. Not until the apartment I'd had near Anthony. I didn't have that anymore, however, and had been moving around a lot again.

"It was what it was." His words were a clear signal to stop the small talk, so instead, I brought up his claim to the throne.

"Which parent provides your link to the throne?" I asked.

"My mother. She's dead now, however."

"My father is mine, and also no longer alive."

"The previous king," Ben added from two seats down. I had Flick and Neritas on either side of me as usual, with Capricia opposite Neritas and one of the city guards on the other side. Brenta was opposite Ben, and she glared at him now.

I stifled the grin that spread across my face and glanced at Grigick. Despite it being a dig toward him, he seemed unconcerned. He was either a cool customer or ready and willing to admit that he wasn't a strong heir to the throne.

"Why try to claim the throne now?" I decided not to beat around the bush. "Do you think you have a stronger claim than I do?"

"Stronger, perhaps not, but you turned it down, as I understand."

"Yes and no. As I said earlier, the people sitting around you convinced me that a monarch wasn't wanted anymore. One of them even stood by and watched as other dragons in the city attacked me, simply for being red. I hope they're protecting you better." As I spoke, his eyes widened and he gulped. It was clearly news to him.

I saw Capricia shift uncomfortably in her seat and was grateful that she was showing some level of discomfort at being called out, even if she wasn't apologetic to me about it.

"Anyway, you didn't answer my question. Why now?"

"Now is when I was asked to. Capricia came to find me."

This confession earned Grigick stares and more than a little anger, but he didn't seem to notice. His gaze remained fixed on me. I got the feeling that this wasn't the conversation he expected and I wasn't acting the way he'd been told I would.

"This is getting us nowhere," Brenta interrupted, bringing the focus to her. "We are crowning Grigick in two days' time and we must insist that the future king be protected by the honor guard and that you return to exile."

"If Scarlet restates her claim to the throne, then the honor guard will not recognize any ceremony you perform for Grigick, and if he's seen as a threat, the guard will do what is necessary to ensure that all dragons bow to the true heir." Alitas spoke very quietly, intent on his drink, then looked up at Brenta.

"You serve whoever is crowned. You don't get to decide who that is." Brenta's voice had grown shrill, and I almost expected her to get to her feet and talk down to Alitas as if he were a naughty child who needed put in his place.

He looked up at her, completely calm as if all she'd done was say his name to bring him into a normal conversation. He took a sip of his soda before bothering to reply.

"You know, you don't get to decide who that is either, Brenta. Detaris might be the seat of the throne, but you're not its gatekeepers. Like me, the elders of all the cities serve their cities and the throne. So I'd calm down if I were you and let Grigick and Scarlet continue their little conversation. Because Scarlet *is* the daughter of the last king. Her mother, his wife, is all the proof the honor guards will ever need to support her claim, and there's nothing that you, Grigick, or anyone else in this building can do or say to change that."

There was a deep silence. Brenta's face changed color, turning a red that an heir might be envious of if it didn't look as if she might explode at any moment. The elder beside her, one of the other men sitting opposite Griffin, very gently placed his hand on her arm.

This seemed to help her calm down. Our meals started to arrive, so I held off my next set of questions and tried to think about where I wanted this to go and what I'd learned. What Detaris wanted was clear. Grigick was their puppet and hadn't wanted the crown himself. But did I want it?

The answer was still no, but I didn't want Capricia and Brenta to lead a monarchy through a puppet king either. They were both too attached to power. But could I stand in their way? Would it divide the dragons further? I didn't need them all, but I didn't want to start a feud, either.

This was going to be a difficult decision, and it was all on my shoulders.

CHAPTER NINE

As we all finished eating and the waitress and chef cleared our plates, I knew I could stall no longer. We had been making polite conversation all through the meal and I'd learned a little about Grigick and the cities he had lived in. There were far more of them than I'd ever thought possible, and I tried to remember as many as I could, but I knew it would be practically impossible.

I told him a little about myself, about being raised in the human world so I would understand them, and how I had been guarded by another dragon until recently. Although I deliberately kept some details vague, I talked as if he knew nothing.

"Capricia has told me that you have fought shadow catchers with her. Is this true?"

"Yes. There's videos of it in the human world. Sometimes I'm recognized."

He raised his eyebrows again, an expression he often used when surprised. I smiled and went to pull out my phone but changed my mind. I wasn't sure I wanted this dragon to see exactly how strong I was. Not right now. And I didn't want to draw attention to what I was when the waitress was around. Ben had said the chef and owner knew what we were, but he had made no mention of the waitress and what she might know.

In front of both of them, no one was saying anything that could give any details away, but they would be gone again soon, and I had to push this meeting along.

As soon as all the plates had been cleared and our chef had let Ben know she and the waitress would be out back if they were needed, the room fell quiet again. Everyone wanted to hear what happened next.

Grigick broke the silence before I could. "I have some questions for you, if you would answer them before you undoubtedly ask me more."

I nodded, willing to listen and explain if it had a chance of helping.

"Why do you want the throne? What made you try and claim it?"

"I don't want it. Not exactly. I care more that it doesn't fall into the wrong hands than I care that I specifically have it. And I care that it is used to unite the dragons and protect this planet. That's why I tried to claim it."

"Because you feel Earth needs protecting?"

"I don't feel it. I know it. The gate needs powering up and the demons that have grown stronger need dealing with and sending back to hell." I felt myself grow more passionate as I spoke, but I didn't stop there. "That's what upset everyone in Detaris so much. They've been teaching everyone that the world is safe and you all just need to live in your cities, but no one has thought to question the oxymoron of just that concept."

It hadn't seemed possible for the room to have grown quieter, but somehow it did. Words were tumbling from my mouth, and it was only as I spoke them that I realized how much sense they made.

"You are all taught to stay in your cities so that there are enough dragons to keep the monster behind the gate, but you are also told that he is stuck there and there's nothing you all need to do. Both cannot be true."

"This is a good point," Grigick replied. "And you say you have been to the gate."

"Yes. It needs powering. It needs a red dragon to repair it and funnel the combined might of the dragons into it."

"And you wish this to be done by whoever leads the dragons."

"It has to be done by whoever leads the dragons, or they're not going to lead for long. I don't think the gate will hold much longer without being strengthened."

Grigick didn't reply for several seconds. He looked thoughtful.

"You didn't tell me of this." He looked at Capricia. "You said that you had been to the gate with Scarlet and that it was a wasteland, but not that it needed dealing with. You spoke of attacks on Detaris and demons appearing in strange places, but not that they are growing stronger."

"This is not all true," Brenta said, but there was an immediate uproar as almost everyone around me came to my defense and spared me the effort.

"It seems that it is true." Grigick looked at me then Brenta. "I won't demand a reason for you telling everyone in the cities that they were safe and nothing needed to be done, but I am disappointed that I was deceived."

Brenta didn't speak, but I saw her tense and turn red again.

"If you wish to know the whole truth of the matter, there's a device in the floor of the elders' chambers. A red dragon and the elders in there can connect to it and you can then tell if anyone in the chamber is lying or not. I've found it very useful on more than one occasion," I said.

"I'm sure Grigick doesn't need to—"

"Brenta, if Grigick is crowned instead of Scarlet, then he has every right to know about all your secrets, and even if he isn't crowned, he deserves to know what he's getting himself into." Griffin once again proved that he wasn't taking any of Brenta's bullshit.

I nodded his way.

"So, if you were king, would you protect Earth?" I asked. "Would you make sure the gate continued to be powered?"

"It seems I would have no choice. It would be a duty, would it not?"

"I would hope that anyone in that position would consider it such." Our eyes met as I spoke, and I thought I saw acknowledgment in his look. We had agreed on something fundamental and he had opted to trust me. That meant a lot if nothing else.

But did I let this guy be the next king? I was pretty sure the decision was mine right now. If I wanted to stop him, I could. And he knew it too.

"I think we all know that this crowning ceremony is being rushed," I said after a pause. "I don't think the general population in Detaris is any more keen on being ruled than they were when the elders made it clear I should step away from it myself. And you don't strike me as someone who can withstand the collective anger they threw at me, which is probably why Capricia and Brenta are trying to get the honor guard for you."

He gave me a nod, but I wasn't sure if he was simply accepting what I said or agreeing with me.

"What do you propose, then?" he asked. It was an implicit nod to me having all the cards and both of us knowing it. Alitas had handed me the reins by insisting he would recognize my claim to the throne above Grigick's, helped a little by the unrest in Detaris that I assumed Brenta and Capricia had stirred against me.

On top of that, I got the impression that Grigick was scared. But I wouldn't divide the dragons if I could help it. And I didn't want a throne.

"I think I need to talk to some of my team before I say for sure." I didn't want to commit to anything at the drop of a hat. "But for now at least, I'm here and I'm sure the honor guard would be okay with protecting both of us for a while. Until we can figure out what's going on."

"That is completely unacceptable," Brenta replied. Capricia looked like she wanted to object, too.

"It's not going to be easy to protect you both unless you're always in the same place," Alitas warned.

"I know. It's a temporary solution that allows everyone to return to Detaris and for our friends and allies to finally rest a little while we figure the rest of this out." I moved to get up and sort out the check. I had no idea how much the bill would be, but I figured that if I didn't have the money for it, Reijo would, or we could split it.

Capricia grabbed my arm across the table, preventing me from moving away if I didn't want to hurt her.

"You're in exile. You can't return to Detaris."

"Look, you can either accept me in Detaris and stop being so antagonistic so your red dragon is protected, or you can refuse to let me in, in which case I will go back to Trellian and I'll call that the new seat of power and have them crown me. Your choice."

"You assume they'll crown you?" Brenta demanded, getting to her feet as well.

Both diplomats from Trellian also stood.

"We've not been asked why we're here yet or our opinions on any of this, but we've seen enough to know that if the honor guard is with Scarlet and everything that has been said here is true, then we're more than happy to also support Scarlet and have our city become the new seat of power. And if it comes with that device that can check if people are lying so we can also see the exact truth of the matter, then we'll soon know if we have made the right decision or not."

It was yet another vote of confidence, but I could see the anger in the dragons in front of me. None of them appreciated having their hands forced and none of them appreciated being threatened. I could understand it, but I had to do what I thought was best for the world as a whole.

"I accept." Grigick stood as well and looked pointedly between Capricia and Brenta. I got the impression this wasn't normal for him, and I appreciated his helping me face the two of them. "For now you can return to Detaris, but only until this matter is sorted to everyone's satisfaction."

Willing to let him feel like this was up to him for a while, I nodded, and Capricia let me go. She could hardly argue with the dragon she was claiming was a suitable king without undermining him, and thankfully she and Brenta understood that on some level and both of them backed off.

It was settled for now.

With nothing else to discuss as a whole group, we called the waitress back and settled the check. Capricia, Reijo, Alitas, and one of the other Detaris elders split the bill four ways to represent the four groups of our party. I was grateful that no one would let me pay, but Reijo insisted he had my cut.

I went back to the door and noticed several helicopters in the sky. They had the familiar patterns of news corporation logos, and nearby was a news van and what looked like a reporter. Although they weren't right by the entrance to the restaurant, I was afraid that we were the subject of their interest.

Had I been recognized?

We came out of the building to a flurry of activity and people pointing us out.

"To the cars, quickly, and no comment on anything to anyone." Alitas ushered me between him, Neritas, and Flick. Almost immediately, more honor guards pulled up around me and some others went to Grigick to hurry him to his vehicle. Most of the city guards tried to copy, protecting whoever was in their delegation in a similar manner.

I grinned at how funny this must have looked to the press, especially as other than myself and the group with me, who had fought shadow catchers, none of the other people being protected would even be recognized.

As I expected, the reporters homed in on me and the vehicle I was heading toward. Ben quickly got into the driver's seat, but Alitas hurried to open the door for me in the back of the car.

The reporter caught up to us as Flick hurried away from me and around to the other side. I heard the reporter call my name as I got inside the car followed by Neritas.

Before he was seated and had shut the door Alitas had run around the car and gotten in the other side. Ben didn't wait for the doors to shut to reverse. The reporter pulled back enough to ensure she didn't get hurt, but the cameraman with her continued to film, crouched slightly to get a good view of us. Neritas lifted his jacket and held it up to block their view of us.

I exhaled as our convoy reformed and we returned to Detaris. Given that we had been located and the helicopters were following us, I half expected to be pulled over by the cops at some point on our journey. It ticked by uneventfully, but I couldn't fully relax. The humans had figured out where I was and we had no way to return to Detaris without making it even easier to find the city. I had blown our secret. It had taken several months and many incidents along the way, but they knew something was up.

The only comfort I had was that I had worked with the police the one time that we'd encountered each other. They'd fought alongside me and we'd come to a handshake agreement that my assistance had been appreciated and I was free to leave. They realized there wasn't a lot they could do to stop me, not after watching me make anything I wished bulletproof.

"Do you think we should find a more discreet route into the city?" I asked everyone in the car with me.

"Even if we did, the rest of the convoy isn't likely to know it, and no matter where we go someone is going to follow us," Ben replied.

Although he had a point, I didn't want to give up on protecting Detaris' location. The dragons in Detaris already blamed me for a lot. I didn't want there to be yet another thing they could be angry at me for.

There was nothing else for it, and everyone agreed. With a helicopter after us and people watching the main entrance, we couldn't prevent the most curious from pinpointing the city anyway. The damage had already been done, and we had to face the consequences.

I felt guilty, but it wasn't all my fault. We were in this together, and the shadow catchers and the way they had relentlessly hunted me had led to this moment.

CHAPTER TEN

It felt strange to be back in Detaris and in the rooms we had been given the last time we were there. They weren't the royal quarters, but they were still spacious enough for the people I considered family. The honor guard had flown up around me, and I had finally had the opportunity to fly again.

It was almost as if we hadn't left, except there were a lot more of us this time. The diplomats from Trellian had also opted to stay with us, and that meant every bedroom was full, and then some. The guards could spread out above and below us, and some of them had agreed to be stationed over in the royal tower with Grigick.

It felt wrong seeing him fly to it, but I'd noticed he didn't fly as well as I did and the rest of the city was as wary of him and stared at him as much as they had me. I may not be accepted in the city and still be considered an outsider, but so was he. It brought me some comfort and removed the sting of seeing him respected by some of the others who had never appeared to like me. Although I knew that I shouldn't get in Grigick's way simply because I was jealous of his living arrangements, I couldn't deny that the temptation was there. I might not feel as if I deserved or ought to have the throne, but I didn't think he did either.

"So, what now?" Alitas asked. "You seemed to have some kind of plan in the restaurant, but you haven't said anything since.

"I'm still in two minds. I don't want to see him as king, but I don't want to get in his way necessarily either. All I want is to see the gate protected. If he will do it, then I see no reason why we shouldn't help him." I shrugged. I wasn't sure I was right, and I knew some of the group with me would want to tell me I was wrong, but I had to do what was best for the planet, not me.

"You really don't want to be queen, do you?" Neritas' anger took me by surprise. "I know you don't want power, but you shouldn't throw the crown away lightly. You have a responsibility, and you can't just walk away from it because you don't want to do anything but see the gate fixed. There's more to the job than powering the gate and fighting demons. Don't be selfish about this."

I frowned, not sure I knew what to say to that, but he got up and walked away before I could try to reassure him. Was he right?

It hurt to be called selfish about not wanting to be a queen. Did the dragon world really need one? But as I thought about it, I knew walking away from it again would leave Brenta in power to some degree. Grigick didn't appear to want to stand up to her and was led by her in terms of information.

"Is there anything we can do to delay this whole thing until the country is safe and we've got a better idea whether Grigick can handle everything?" I asked. "I want to step away knowing it's all in good hands."

"You could demand that there's a period for him to prove that he's a better fit than you, and if he does you'll officially abdicate," Alitas said, although I got the impression that he didn't like the idea much. "But I don't doubt that they'll want the honor guard for him. And I imagine he's going to need it."

"Especially if I do demand that he fixes and powers up the gate."

"We've barely begun making progress in that regard, and I don't feel comfortable giving what we've been working on to a dragon I don't trust." Jace spoke her mind, as usual. "Anthony worked hard to get the trust of Sarai, me, Cios, and Elias, and by virtue of you and Ben being people he trusted, we've given you enough opportunity to prove we can trust you as well. Our group won't feel the same about Grigick. Especially not when he's someone Capricia chose and Brenta is backing."

"I confess to feeling similar." Griffin frowned and I could almost see the warring thoughts and disappointment in his mind. He was an elder who had served alongside Brenta for many years before she pushed him away without a care for his safety.

Everyone was silent as I tried to digest what everyone was saying. Neritas was still gone and I felt a strong pull to go after him. His words stung, and I didn't want him to think I didn't care. But I had no idea what I was doing. Grigick had lived in so many dragon cities that he would inherently have a better understanding of what the dragon world needed.

"So, if I claim the throne, we'll go to Trellian and possibly have a dragon civil war on our hands. If I don't claim the throne, Grigick takes it, and the honor guard and the gate and the fate of the world are in his hands."

"You can't take the chance he'll do the right thing," Jace said immediately. "You have to claim the throne."

"Not right away, though. Delaying Grigick and making the gate safe gives you time. Time to get support if you do intend to take the throne, and time to focus on one task at once." Alitas leaned in closer. "But we'd have to protect him and I don't have enough well-trained honor guard to protect the two of you unless both of you are in the same place, especially given that some of the guards I'm working with right now are saying I have to give my allegiance to whoever is most likely to be heir."

I tilted my head to the side as I thought about what he'd said. As long as the two of us were in the same place, we could both be protected.

"What if I joined the honor guard temporarily?" I asked a few seconds later, voicing the thought as soon as it popped into my head.

"That...would be interesting." Alitas sat back, thinking for a moment.

"That's crazy, surely. You'd have to protect him." Ben got up and started pacing.

"I'd have to do what's needed to protect the throne and to power the gate, right?" I looked at Alitas.

"Yes. You'd have to obey orders—from me."

"What about Brenta and Capricia? And Grigick?"

"Technically you would answer to me and not to them. I would answer to Grigick in that case. If you joined the honor guard in the interest of giving Grigick time to prove himself, I could keep you safe and serve him for now. We could make it a probationary period and I could enforce that for you when the time comes."

"If this is truly the option you wish to go for, then Trellian and Isethnore would support you, but for the sake of informing the elders in our city, we would wish to witness Grigick's attempts to fix the gate." Liam gave me a nod. It was one of the first things he had said during this entire incident, but I appreciated it.

It was another indication that we might make a better case once I'd had time to gather more allies and prove Grigick wasn't good enough. And I disliked the idea of being in charge so much that if Grigick was good, I'd hand power over when he had managed everything of importance.

"Okay, that's decided then." I got up, surveying the room and the myriad faces. I could tell not everyone thought it was a perfect idea, but they weren't arguing with me. "I'm going to talk to Neritas and then we should go to the elders and get Grigick to agree to this as well."

Despite my intention for everyone else to stay where they were, Flick came with me, hanging back a little as I went to the back room in the direction Neritas had gone. I found him standing by one of the large windows looking out over the city.

"Hey." I moved closer and Flick shut the door behind us all.

"I'm sorry," he replied, not missing a beat. "I know this is hard for you."

"And for both of you. I'm not a perfect person, and there's a lot standing against us."

"That doesn't mean I should have called you selfish."

"Doesn't mean you're wrong. You're definitely right that there's a lot more to being in charge than just defending this gate. There's so much more that needs to be dealt with, especially with the human world working out that we exist." I sat on the edge of the bed as he turned away from the window.

Over the next few minutes, I told them the rough plan and what I thought might happen, and why I'd decided that.

"Sounds like it could really piss Brenta off. She wants us gone from the city, but wants the honor guard to stay and protect her stooge, and you're one of them. Love it!"

I grinned as Neritas summed it up. Almost immediately his eyes started to twinkle. Both of us were more than happy to piss Brenta off. And it meant that I still had his support.

"It makes sense for Flick and I to continue being honor guards, then, for now, as well."

"For now. We can all leave together if this doesn't go the way we want and claim the throne. Assuming Grigick agrees, anyway."

"If he's got any sense, he will." Flick got up and moved over to the door for me.

With my party in agreement, we went back out to the others. I paused to look around the room. Some more of the honor guards had come back, satisfied that Grigick was safe for now and wanting to get additional orders, but everyone stopped and looked at me when I walked in.

The group before me had joined me so gradually that I hadn't truly taken in how much support I had from how many powerful dragons. I could achieve a lot if I set my mind to it, and I had unsettled the balance of control and power that had existed in the dragon world already. It gave me a sense of confidence and the knowledge that I wasn't just some nobody from LA, and it allowed me the strength I needed to carry on.

"Let's go talk to the elders. Alitas, can you get Grigick and meet us in the chambers with him, please?" I kept my request polite, but I knew what I wanted.

"As long as at least half the honor guard goes with you, then, yes." He shot me a wink that made it clear I was going to be protected by him whether I liked it or not and certain orders were only going to be obeyed to a degree.

It was an interesting position for him to hold, whichever way you thought about it. It made me wonder what it was like to be one of the few people on the planet who could willfully disobey a command from their superior if it endangered said superior.

Not wanting to think about it but grateful that it was going to be to my advantage over this next stage, I waited for everyone else to be ready before I led my small procession up to the council chambers. I had an offer to make, and if they understood anything I did, they were quickly going to realize they had no choice but to accept it.

The elders didn't look pleased to see us when I landed and morphed back into human form. I strode inside anyway, grateful that Griffin had come with me and stuck close by. Since being exiled as well, he'd become a self-appointed diplomat for my party, and I appreciated it more than I could put into words.

"Gather the rest of the elders and Grigick and anyone else he feels ought to be present," I ordered. For now, I was in charge. Until I confirmed otherwise, I was the potential heir to the throne and had the honor guard's support.

The glares I received grew more obvious, but Griffin passed on the command to the staff nearby and Alitas soon landed with Grigick anyway. He came in and gave me a respectful nod. I returned the gesture, grateful that he was acknowledging me and doing so respectfully when several of the others weren't.

"You had your discussion faster than I was expecting," Grigick said as he sat on a small chair to one side. He immediately insisted everyone get seated comfortably.

Once more, I felt grateful that I had the diplomat on my side and that he was going to do everything he could to help me make this work.

As soon as I was sitting opposite Grigick and everyone had gathered around, I noticed the elders came closer and we had more of an informal gathering than the usual experience I'd had in these chambers. In the past, I had stood in the center with all eyes on me or Ben while we were grilled, and we had skirted the lines of truth and tried to omit anything we thought would cause more trouble than it was worth.

Now we were sitting around on an equal footing with everybody else, trying to work out what to do. For the most part. Capricia remained standing a little behind and to one side of Grigick as if she was protecting him from some unknown threat, and Brenta had insisted that her ornately carved elder's chair be brought to the center of the room instead of using one of the plainer ones the rest of us were sitting on.

"Thank you for all taking the time to figure this out with us," I began. "I know this is a very difficult matter and it impacts a lot of dragons and humans."

"For some of us, this matter is simple, but you continue to complicate everything," Brenta broke in.

Several people gasped, and Neritas stepped forward along with Ben, Alitas, and my mother to give her a piece of their minds.

I held my hand out. "It's okay," I said just loud enough that they would hear me. Louder, I went on, "I think it is already clear to all of you that the throne is mine to claim or hand over. As much as some of you wish to crown Grigick instead of me, the honor guard and dragons of other cities, as well as many from Detaris, do support me."

"So you would insist that we bow to you?" Capricia glared at me.

"No. But I would insist that you prove Grigick is the better option. Genetic inheritance and hereditary leadership have never appealed to me. I don't think that I should become the queen just because I was born in the right family. But if another is a better option, then I want to be convinced before I will step out of the way."

"You cannot stop us from crowning him." Brenta sat forward as if this settled the matter.

"No, but if you did, I would go to Trellian, have them crown me, and it would start a civil war between Detaris and everyone who did support me. And I would have the honor guard and almost every other dragon in this room by my side. Is that what you want, Brenta?"

The elders connected to the device underneath the floor and read the truth in my statements. I would do it. I'd already decided that I would do what was needed to stop the wrong person from being crowned.

"What would you propose Grigick did to prove to you?" one of the other elders asked.

"I would have the crowning held off until Grigick has sealed the gate again and dealt with the worst of the shadow catcher threat. If he can gather enough of the right dragons, work with my contacts to fix the gate, and harness the power of the dragon community, then he will have proven himself worthy of the throne."

"And give you time to remove him permanently and gain more support and subvert him?" Brenta looked as if she wanted to spit at my feet.

"As a token of goodwill and support, I will give him the honor guard, and everyone with me will be encouraged to work with him to aid in this endeavor. He'll have no fewer resources than I do."

There were a few gasps at this, but Grigick nodded.

"I accept," he said before anyone could object. "I will fix this gate. Whether it is truly in danger of failing or not, we cannot take that chance. Not when so many lives are at stake."

I exhaled, feeling myself relax for the first time in ages. The gate would be protected, one way or another.

CHAPTER ELEVEN

Despite the progress I had made, I couldn't sleep. Instead, I was sitting by the window of my tower room watching the sun rise over Detaris and wondering if I had done the right thing.

It was too late, though. There was nothing else to be done. I had made an offer and it had been accepted. I needed to see it through to the end.

But that didn't stop me from being scared. After Grigick had accepted my offer, I returned to the tower and Alitas took the majority of his honor guard to the other tower while he worked out how to better protect us both. Everything else had been put off to today, and I had a feeling there were going to be more questions and demands.

Unlike the previous time I was living in this tower, no one was catering to our needs. We spent the rest of the evening sorting out food arrangements and making sure everyone had a place to sleep.

Grigick had stayed in his tower, and Alitas had

returned later in the evening and informed me that he'd need me to start being an honor guard today, which would allow me and Grigick to be in the same place. I was both nervous and eager.

I wanted to see what the other red dragon was like and have the chance to get to know him better and see what he might be capable of. I also wanted to check what he knew already and if he knew about any red dragon powers or abilities that I didn't. An exchange of information would hopefully benefit us both.

Neritas knocked on the door and gently opened it a few minutes after the sun was fully in the sky.

He walked over to me. "Couldn't sleep either?"

"No. Too much riding on today. I need to make sure this works and we get this gate sealed, and I'm not sure how any of them are going to react to me being an honor guard."

"They'll probably take it the same way they've taken everything. Brenta and Capricia will hate it because it was your idea. A bunch of others will be too scared to speak out either way, and the rest will support you in one way or another."

I grinned at his description. It was apt enough.

"Okay, let's get breakfast and then to our duties."

Alitas had scheduled Flick and Neritas with me as well, trusting them to protect me as I protected Grigick, and we'd been given a brief overview and training. On top of that, Alitas or his second-in-command would always be nearby whenever I was on duty.

Flick flew in with breakfast, Reijo and Ben with him, and moved to the dining area. They'd managed to get several large platters of bacon, pancakes, scrambled eggs, and a huge jug of maple syrup from one of the restaurants. It was the perfect breakfast for the day we were going to have.

I tucked in as more of my friends and family woke up and came to join us. I could detect a hint of unease from many of them. Today was going to be new for all of us and something we had to work through.

As soon as I and the guards who were coming with me had finished eating, I got up and gathered my belongings. I made sure I had my shield, sword, and the armor that Alitas had found for me.

I'd requested to have a look in the vault where Neritas had found the sword and shield, but we'd been refused access. Although Neritas had gotten in there in the past, he didn't feel as if he could attempt to sneak in this time. If he got caught, it could blow our entire plan out of the window. As it was, Brenta wanted to send us back into exile now that we'd opted to give Grigick a chance.

By the time I was ready, so were my companions, and we flew to the tower. It felt good to fly, however briefly. Plenty of other dragons were in the air around the tower, many of them were the black dragons of the city guard. I had never had so many in the air around me when I had been residing there.

It didn't take us long to get there, but when I landed I noticed that Brenta and Capricia were already there, along with several others. They did not look pleased to see me.

I smiled at them nonetheless but hung back as Alitas took the lead and asked us all to fan out and take our positions around the internal structure.

"Scarlet, you can stay in here with Grigick. That seems the best all-around and gives you two the safest area to keep track of.

"Scarlet can't stay here. She's still under exile and we're having an important meeting."

"Then you'll have to have your important meeting in Scarlet's presence. I've given her an order and I expect her to carry it out. She's also now immune to any laws but the laws of the honor guard as policed by me, which means you can't exile her from any city or element of the dragon world, as you can't order any other honor guard around."

Brenta gaped as Capricia laughed.

"Well played, Red," Capricia said a few seconds later. "I wondered how you were going to get around that hurdle."

"This way I can see that the job I'm here for gets done, and I can make sure that there's always a line of red dragons available to keep us all safe." I shrugged as if that should have been obvious, and Brenta turned a wonderful shade of red again.

"I am in need of food. Perhaps we can continue this meeting later, anyway," Grigick suggested, but I noticed his eyes shifted between the two powerful women on either side of him.

I got the impression that despite how he had appeared to negotiate with me and had agreed to terms that Capricia and Brenta might not have done, he was still very much under their thumb and intimidated by them.

Brenta seemed to accept for now that she couldn't do anything. Alitas was standing beside me and telling her she had no choice. It wasn't me being awkward directly, it was the leader of the honor guard, and she needed to get along well with him if she was going to be included in Grigick's life.

I almost envied the power Alitas had but I could also see the responsibility he carried now more than ever. He had to juggle a lot of unknowns and his life was constantly in danger.

As soon as the two powerful women had left, Alitas gave me a nod and Neritas and Flick took up their positions. It left me alone with Grigick. I smiled at him and went to the window not too far from him to look out. I wanted to take my duty seriously, and I knew that Alitas thought it important to check all entrances and exits to a room.

When dragons could fly and transform as they did, large windows were practically doors. It was up to me to make sure no one else came in here unless Grigick allowed it, and I didn't think they were a danger.

When Alitas explained to me that I could overrule Grigick on certain things if I thought what he wanted to do was too dangerous, including meeting with certain people, I was tempted to use it to keep Brenta and Capricia away from him, but there were better ways to achieve that. I just needed to give Grigick time.

"Everything looks safe enough for now," I said a minute or so later when I had checked everything Alitas had instructed me to.

"Thank you, I guess. Though I must confess that this feels very unusual."

"Alitas assured me that other red dragons were honor guards in the past, especially when there were plenty of us."

"This does not surprise me, but there are just the two of

us—that we know of—and we have barely met." He looked at me as if he held the command of the room, his head up straight and his shoulders back, but I could see the fear in his eyes.

"Then would it help if we got to know each other a little? I meant what I said yesterday. If you can do what's needed, I'm happy to back down and leave you alone. And I wouldn't have joined the honor guard if I didn't think I could offer you my protection in the meantime."

"I guess I shall have to trust that for now." He still didn't look entirely at ease, but he went over to the table laden with food.

"You don't have to trust me. I'm capable of earning that trust."

This gained me a raised eyebrow, but he didn't reply, focusing on getting himself breakfast. I was glad I'd eaten already as he piled his plate high. He didn't offer me any and I didn't ask. Instead, I kept my eye on all the entrances and exits, knowing Alitas would check in with me and the others regularly.

"Are you going to stand around awkwardly the entire time you're in here?" he asked.

I frowned, not realizing I had been showing my discomfort. I had been trying to hide it and just do my job while I calmed down and figured out how to begin a conversation.

Grigick sat back as soon as he'd finished eating and looked over at me again.

"I'm sorry that I got in the way of you being crowned," I said, meaning it. I knew enough of what it felt like to be about to be crowned and then have everything go wrong.

"I get the feeling that this gate matters to you."

"Not letting the planet die matters to me."

"That is a noble goal. And it will remain to be seen if you let me have the throne after."

"I will. If the gate is protected."

"So you say. You had best tell me what you know. Brenta thinks this is all a big bluff and Capricia is being as guarded with what she says as she is with me."

"You're their hope of keeping power. But Capricia has seen everything I have with only a few exceptions."

Over the next hour, I told him about the gate. I described it, the difficulty of getting to it, and the need to power it up to reduce the circle of rot and the brokenness of the pillars. It led naturally to talking about Jace, Elias, and Sarai and how much I trusted them.

"They're good dragons. They just don't like living in the cities with the current rules and limitations, and they don't think we should hide from the shadow catchers but fight them."

"I can understand some of that for sure."

"They have been invaluable. I have learned a lot from them, and they've fought beside me on more than one occasion."

"I've seen some of the videos now. Jace and Capricia are...scary."

"Tell me about it. I don't like crossing either of them." I grinned and it broke some of the tension.

We had agreed on something for the first time in a way that helped us bond. I let the moment linger, the awkwardness reduced enough that it didn't hurt.

"So, what do you know of our part in powering the

gate?" I asked. I was pretty sure Capricia would have gone over that but wanted to be certain. He hadn't asked, so I didn't want to assume. I might be able to get an idea of what red dragon magic he knew of at the same time. Or at least begin that conversation.

"It needs filling up and only royal red dragons can do it. Pretty simple." He picked up his plate and went back to the table for more food.

I frowned again, feeling like he was shutting down the conversation, and I tried to think of anything that could keep it going again. He wasn't wrong about it. Something didn't sit right with me either.

"It might be worth you training with me and the others so you are able to fight shadow catchers too before you go to the gate," I added a few seconds later.

"Is there going to be time? You and your friends seem very eager for me to go."

"I think there's a mix of reasons why we're eager. We don't know how long we have, and Brenta and Capricia both know that the sooner you go and deal with the gate, the sooner you can become the king they want."

"That's a good point. And so we ought to pack, should we not?"

"I'm pretty much always ready to go. I'm just waiting on you and your team. If you're confident you can handle it, we can leave."

A frown crossed his face at my challenge. I shrugged to make it seem less antagonistic, but I feared the damage was done already. I still didn't know if he knew anything about how to use his powers. He had once again avoided talking about it and deflected.

I spent the next few hours watching him in silence until Capricia came back and confirmed that we would make our way to the gate the following day. Jace and her team had made some progress with the gate and wanted to go back there and see if their prototype replacement for the pillars might work.

By the time my shift for the day was done, I was more than a little bored. There had been no danger to Grigick and no one had come to bother him about anything. We'd talked a little more as I tried to find confirmation one way or another that he knew about red dragons' abilities or anything else about being a red dragon and heir, but I got nowhere. I might as well have been talking to any random dragon from another city.

Trying to be friendly no matter what, I'd got him talking about some of the cities he'd enjoyed visiting, but it was hard work, and after a while, silence reigned again.

As I went back to my tower, I collapsed into a chair in the dining room, grateful that someone had fetched dinner.

Alitas wasn't far behind me, then Flick and Neritas also sat. Jace came into the room only a few seconds later and nodded at us.

"You all look like you've had as shit a day as I have." She frowned before grabbing a stack of plates and adding food to all of them.

Appreciating the gesture, I kept silent so she could talk.

"Getting the idiots that call themselves the elders of this city to recognize something important when you're trying to tell them until you're blue in the face is not my idea of fun."

"I take it the meeting about fixing the pillars didn't go well?" Ben asked as he joined us.

Jace shook her head.

"Tomorrow is going to be an interesting day, that's for sure."

CHAPTER TWELVE

It felt strange to be in Detaris and flying down to the cars with my pack again. After being kicked out I'd never have thought I'd be doing this again, but here I was.

We had to use an insane number of vehicles, and a helicopter of the same news channel hovered in the distance as if they were now always there trying to get images of us. I leaned toward Ben as we put supplies into the trunk.

"Do you know what the humans are saying about us lately?" I asked, having not thought about it since we'd entered Detaris and I'd been playing honor guard and trying to make nice with Grigick.

"There's still a lot who don't believe the videos of us are any more than a hoax, but there's others who are interested. Local news is focusing on us, and those with nothing better to do with their time."

I nodded, grateful for the information. There wasn't going to be any hiding us at this rate, but I still hoped we could avoid them finding out about us for some time. I could only keep going and try to work out how to avoid them as much as possible.

If the human world found out about us while we were doing what we needed to protect them, then it would have to happen. I wasn't going to stop protecting them just to stop them from discovering dragons. Many still did not believe we existed, which was a huge help. At the very least, it bought us more time.

"I think it would be better if Scarlet and her friends remained here while we went about this mission," Capricia said as she came closer to our car and saw my usual pack on my back. "She draws the attention of the humans and their news reporters."

"Scarlet is coming whether that's true or not," Alitas shot back. "She's needed and you know it."

Capricia shook her head. "This mission is happening under my authority, and I refuse to allow her here when it puts the rest of the group in more danger."

"This is very simple, Capricia. Is Grigick going on this mission?" Alitas stopped what he was doing and turned to face the city guard captain.

"Of course he is. We need his red dragon abilities."

"Then I have the authority over his honor guard, and our best fighter against the shadow catchers as well as the one with the most experience is Scarlet. She's coming with us, and you know that makes sense on a lot of different levels."

Capricia pursed her lips and looked at me as if she was going to ask me not to. I stepped forward.

"I know you don't like me, but I want to kill shadow catchers and we both know that I'm really good at it. My experience is worth the risk from curious humans. On top of that, I need to see this for myself and teach Grigick a few things along the way. If you want him to be king, then you need to have me there as well as him."

This had more of an impact than Alitas' attempts to get me to be accepted and I was finally allowed to get into one of the cars. To appease Brenta and Capricia, I wasn't traveling too close to Grigick, but farther back in the convoy and with my usual group. It meant that other honor guards would be protecting him, but everyone knew I didn't need their protection as much out in the human world.

I had a feeling we'd all end up in one group at our destination anyway.

"Everyone ready?" Ben asked. He was our designated driver again.

"As ready as we're going to be for whatever this trip might be," Alitas replied. "Jace thinks it's going to be a shitshow and I don't really disagree with that assessment."

"We'll see," I suggested. "I'm not sure how much Grigick knows about red dragon powers. When it comes to everything that needs to be done to fight the shadow catchers and power the gate, he was cagey, and although he knew he had to do it, he didn't seem to want to talk about it."

The car was silent.

"This could be real fun," Neritas said dryly.

I wasn't going to argue with him, but I hoped we would both be wrong.

"If he really has no clue, it changes a lot. He's going to be a huge liability and you're going to have to rescue him, Scarlet," Alitas added.

"Is that an order as an honor guard?" I asked. "'Cause a

small part of me is tempted to let him fend for himself. I'm sure there are more deserving dragons I could be saving if it came to it."

"I can make it an order if I need to," he replied as if he was serious but I saw him grinning in the rearview mirror.

We didn't get to say more to each other before we were driving out of the city and the barrier that kept us hidden from the humans was behind us. Immediately the folks camped out nearby were on their feet and filming again, no doubt trying to get an idea of why they could see the entrance to the city but never quite find it.

"We're really going to have to do something about these people," Ben said as he followed the car in front.

"I'd say the elders are open to suggestions, but I get the feeling that they'd just discount anything that came from us simply because it's us suggesting it." I sighed, wishing it wasn't true.

I watched the humans from the safety of the middle in the back seat, hoping they wouldn't notice me, but we were in the same vehicle as always. We probably should have changed, but I doubted anyone in Detaris was going to lend us another one.

They weren't going to help us with avoiding being chased, but it was also to their detriment. The helicopters soon came overhead and followed us as we drove.

"We're going to need to lose them somehow," I said ten minutes later with the drone of the flying annoyances beginning to grate on me.

"That's not going to be easy unless they both run low on fuel at the same time." Ben frowned as he spoke and glanced up at them.

Alitas didn't respond but pulled out his phone.

"I might know someone who can get them off our tail for a bit. But it's going to cost a huge favor and I don't like owing anyone."

"Hold off for now, then. They might get bored when they realize that we're just going to be driving most of the day."

"As long as they don't bother us at our chosen dinner location." Flick leaned toward the window to look up at the helicopter on the other side. We'd already planned our travel for the day and I knew Brenta and Capricia would be seething that they were following us when they'd specifically asked for me to stay behind so that we wouldn't attract attention.

None of this was going according to plan, despite how much of what I was asking for or insisting upon I was getting. There was always something else. Something I forgot or didn't expect. I often had to replan and backtrack and think on my feet to deal with it. I got the feeling that it was always going to be like this to some degree.

I tried not to worry about it, instead talking to Alitas about how we were going to handle the walk to the gate. We had more dragons with us than before, and Elias, Sarai, and several more would meet us in the usual parking lot. Having the extra power was useful, but it also came with challenges of its own.

More dragons meant more to protect if shadow catchers came. And I had no idea if Grigick could fight or not.

"We'll have to assume he can't and reshuffle if he can," Alitas said when I pointed that out. "Which means you're taking the lead on the way there with your usual group. I'll stick by him and make use of the city guard and anyone you can help charge up. We'll have to put your mom in the back to help stop attacks from behind."

"Until we're on our way back from the gate."

"Hopefully by then it will be stronger and we won't have so far to go."

I didn't reply, I didn't want to trust that hope, but I couldn't do anything else. It was the best and only plan we had. We were doing what we could, and we had the best resources I was likely to get in a hurry.

With any luck, this recharge would at least keep the gate holding long enough to come back and do more. But luck had a habit of running out at the most awkward times, and I wasn't going to leave anything to luck that I didn't have to.

Thankfully, the helicopters had to back off after a while. I doubted it would be the last we saw of them, though.

Even when we stopped to eat, no one came back to us.

Alitas got out of the car as soon as we could park and eat. We chose a small country area, planning to get back on the road as a convoy as soon as all our drivers had eaten. No one wanted to waste any time, and I was willing to cooperate with Brenta and Capricia as they set the tone for the journey and urged us all on again.

If I was going to make this work, I needed to cooperate and let them be queen bees for now. Then I would have more latitude to do what was needed when it was really needed. I kept my head down and let Alitas take the lead for a while, listening as he talked to Capricia and Brenta.

"I need everyone to be very careful once we get there, and prepared for the mind games this demon plays. We can't be too slow or struggle the way we have in the past." Alitas looked pointedly at Capricia, but she lifted her head as if this wasn't something she had ever done.

"We have some of the best dragons from Detaris with us. I assure you that there won't be any problems," Brenta replied. I got the feeling that she had no idea what was coming.

Alitas clenched his fists and looked at Grigick, ignoring both women to focus on the red dragon.

"It will focus on you most. It already knows it can't make Scarlet and Sienna turn around, but you're another red and it doesn't know you. You're going to have it talk to you and distract you and make you doubt yourself. You'll need to just keep putting one foot in front of the other and focus. Can you do that?"

"Of course he can," Capricia replied for Grigick. "He's one of the royal line. This is in his blood as much as it is in Scarlet's."

I stifled a grin at hearing the last words. She'd inadvertently acknowledged that I knew what I was doing, and also that my claim to the throne was valid, but whether Grigick took as naturally to it or not remained to be seen. One thing was for sure. We were going to find out very soon.

It didn't take long for the drivers to finish eating while I listened to Alitas tell Grigick about the route to the gate. He had information that I didn't, having spent years in its vicinity, watching it when he thought there might never be another red dragon to protect us all.

"The hardest part is right before you get to the border of the rot. It's like he concentrates all his mental malice there. But inside the rot, he can speak in your head without it seeming to drain him. Outside it, he only seems to be able to do that some of the time."

I exhaled, making a mental note to ask Alitas more about that if I got the chance. I hadn't spoken about the voices very much or what they said to me, but Alitas had made it clear I wasn't the only one hearing them and that there was a pattern to it. It was useful information.

Before he could say much more, we were ushered back into the cars and back on our way, and our next stop was the parking lot itself. By then we would have almost a hundred dragons, and a significant chunk of them would be green and black. The rest would be some of the most powerful dragons of the other colors.

I got the impression from what everyone was saying that this was going to be the biggest joint mission any of the dragons had undertaken in a long time. And I was a big part of it.

CHAPTER THIRTEEN

As the parking lot came into sight, my stomach knotted painfully. I was more than a little nervous. If we didn't do this carefully, a lot of dragons could die.

Everyone we were meeting was already there. They moved out of the way as our entire convoy pulled up, and I saw Elias raise an eyebrow when Grigick got out of the car.

Alitas took charge immediately, not letting Brenta or Capricia dictate too much before he got everyone organized into a line of dragons in pairs. He spaced everyone out and got me near the front as he had intended.

"Of course, you've got Scarlet out at the front like she's leading this," Capricia protested. "Do we need to remind you that Grigick is the dragon we're all following right now?"

"The gate is what I have experience with, so we are going to do this the way I think is best," Alitas shot back. "I want to keep all of you alive, and from this moment on a demon is going to be planning to kill as many of us as possible. If you can't follow my orders, you can get back in the cars and stay here or go back to Detaris. Is that clear?"

I'd never seen Alitas look so severe in all the time I'd known him. Grigick put his hand on Capricia's shoulder.

"I would trust my honor guard on this. As he says, he has been here far longer than any of us. He knows our enemy best and I will see for myself soon enough to know if we can trust him or not."

It was a very honest appraisal of the situation. I had to hand it to him for being so level-headed about it, but that still didn't mean he could handle this trip.

With this minor power struggle dealt with, we got into position. I reached gently for the connection with all the different dragons in the group, focusing on the dragons closest to me. I soon had the sword and shield I carried fully charged.

I pulled a little more from everyone and charged up every shield and weapon in the group. I noticed Grigick wasn't doing anything. No magic flowed to him or from him, so I connected to him as well, locking eyes with him.

He appeared to hold his breath for a few seconds, and I tried to show him what I was doing through our connection, giving him magic I'd taken but also pulling from him into the shield he carried so he'd hopefully feel that connection. Although it was disappointing that he didn't know how to do it, I hoped he would learn.

Slowly, he tried to take over. He was clumsy and I felt him struggling to connect to others, so I guided the mental tendrils of energy until he was connected in his own right. I backed off as he pulled a little more energy from the dragons around him. They were almost all Detaris dragons, and more black than any other color, but it gave him the opportunity to learn.

I nodded to Alitas to let him know I was ready and we were all as prepared as we could be. Mom had already taken care of some of the back of the group. Her skills had improved since we had been together. Training and having another red dragon around had been good for both of us.

"All right, everyone stay with your partner and a good distance from those in front. Communicate if you're struggling, but whatever you do, don't stop walking." Alitas hit the hilt of his spear against his shield and gave me the signal to get going.

Knowing this was going to be more of a marathon than a sprint, I traveled along the path at a steady but still fairly casual walking pace. Most of the dragons in Detaris were in good shape, but we had Griffin and Brenta with us, as well as Elias and Sarai, and none of them were young anymore. We couldn't leave them behind.

Alitas had made sure they were also well protected and within the group sensibly. Elias and Sarai were not too far behind me, and Griffin and Brenta were near my mother, where she could help them and they wouldn't bother me too much. Capricia was near Grigick. Alitas was letting her act as some of his protection.

In this situation, I acted as my own protection better than anyone else could, but I still had some of the more powerful green dragons and a variety of colors near me. I had been careful where I had pulled the magic from, not taking from the green dragons, and I monitored how they were doing as I went.

I spread my mind out to feel for the demon's minions.

They'd been suspiciously absent in my mind on our journey over here. The city hadn't had them around in as high numbers as it had in the past, possibly because I'd killed so many of them in that area only a few weeks earlier, but there were still usually plenty here.

Of course, I'd also been hunting them from the lake nearby when I had been living on the yacht. I could have reduced the numbers in the area more than I'd thought. For now, I could only feel the great evil that lay ahead of us and the distant movement of a few shadow catchers here and there, almost like sentries.

We carried on walking for half an hour before a ripple of discontent moved up the group. I had felt the weight growing in my body and knew I wouldn't be the only one. I glanced back to see that the group had spread out a little too much. Following the last instructions I'd had, I slowed, but I didn't stop. I felt back down the group and noticed that the biggest gaps lay between Grigick and the guards he followed and Brenta and Jace. The two dragons barely moved.

I pushed a little energy into Brenta, assuming her age was what was getting to her, but I had no idea what was going on with Grigick. He was young and had been informed of what to expect. Was he buckling under the mental weight already?

Considering what was happening behind me and still slowly prodding the group forward, I watched my party as they started to catch up and get back into formation, except for Grigick. He just got slower and slower. Frowning, I turned to Neritas, who had been walking beside me for the whole journey so far and carrying the shield he'd stolen in one of our battles with a handler.

"Keep everyone going forward at this pace and whatever you do, don't stop. I'll be back as soon as I've figured out what Grigick is playing at."

Neritas nodded, tiredness in his eyes but his jaw set in determination. I pushed a little more energy into him and focused on keeping our connection to support him as I turned and walked back down the side of the group.

As I went, I offered words of encouragement to all the dragons struggling past and Elias patted me on the shoulder.

"You're a strong woman to have faced this more than once."

"It gets easier," I replied without thinking. Somewhere along the way, it had done just that. I remembered the advice Alitas had given me the first time when it had felt impossible. I was grateful it was easier now that I was going against that advice and not focusing on moving forward but walking away again for a while. I was pretty sure progressing again was going to be more difficult.

I fell in beside Grigick, taking his arm as I did so I could get close. The connection between us was still strong and he still had plenty of magic in him, so I didn't pump in more, but something was wrong. He slumped onto me, the weight of his frame almost crushing me and slowing me as well.

"What's getting to you?" I whispered as I tried to keep him moving.

At the same time Capricia, struggling on the other side

of him, fell back a little. I tried not to worry about her as Grigick tried to stop.

I didn't let him. I held him tightly and practically dragged him with me.

"Come on, Grigick. You want to be king. You've got to find a deeper strength."

"How? This is a weight too great to bear." His voice was low and tired and showed the strain in his mind.

"You're a red dragon, right?" I asked.

"Yes. I am, but—"

"No, buts. You've got a strength in you that no other color has. You're going to be a bigger target to the demon ahead because he knows that you're a bigger threat. But you also have more strength."

Grigick didn't reply, but his next step seemed to have more confidence in it, and he took the next and the next without making me feel as if I was dragging him along. I had no idea what to do now. His arm was still around me as I supported him.

"I get through this by counting my steps and just focusing on that. Blocking everything else out. Because it gets easier. As soon as you're most of the way there and by the edge of the decay, the weight lifts right off."

That wasn't the total truth. The weight just didn't seem as bad because there was something else to focus on when you got to the decay. And progress toward the center slowed considerably. Inside the field of decay, I'd always been so focused on ignoring the voice in my head and helping channel magic where it was needed that I didn't have anything else distracting me. I had no idea for sure if it really got easier or not.

"This is not what I expected when you said it was like wading through molasses." Grigick sighed and leaned more heavily on me.

I had struggled with the walk—I hadn't been warned of what to expect, but I had still made it through. This dragon had support and a warning and was meant to be a better choice of heir than me. It would be almost funny if I wasn't aware of how important it was to get us all to the gate and strengthen it.

"Come on, Grigick. Pull yourself together. Do you think this is any easier on me?" I asked, trying another strategy but keeping my voice low so it wouldn't be overheard. "Are you really going to make me look this much better than you in front of all these dragons?"

"You've faced this before."

"Yes. And without warning, support, or understanding. You know this is just a psychological attack and yet you still aren't shaking it off. And besides, it doesn't matter how many times I've done this. They'll see me not only appearing to not struggle at all but also able to help you, and they'll see you struggling more than anyone else here. For your sake, you have to pull yourself together and fight this."

This seemed to lend him a little strength again. I had no idea what he thought of me for saying it.

"That's it. Now you're getting the hang of it," I added when he started to get into a plodding rhythm. At the same time, I eased my grip on his side.

He kept going, taking more of his weight, and I started counting just loud enough for him to hear. It took him a little while, but eventually, he joined in, and he finally let go of me, walking beside me rather than leaning on me.

The look of strain and weary defeat remained on his face, but he kept plodding forward and I was free to focus on keeping going myself. It wasn't easy, and I was also feeling the strain. My legs felt heavy and my body felt drained of all energy, but I needed to move back into position next to Neritas.

Whether it was the pressure of being in front and leading the way, or if whatever was out there was attacking him more, I could see Neritas starting to flag, and I cared about him a lot more than Grigick. If the red dragon who wanted to take the throne couldn't keep his shit together, I wasn't going to do any more to help him.

It was harsh of me in some ways, but this journey was in part to see if he was good enough to lead. And so far I wasn't impressed.

I wasn't impressed at all.

Making my way back up the line was tougher than I expected it to be. The weight of the mental battle started to hit me as soon as I passed the first dragon and I had to keep pushing myself faster than the dragons beside me to get back to Neritas before it grew too much for him.

All of this was almost too much, and I was also aware of the scrutiny. As much as I had told Grigick that everyone was watching him to see if he measured up to me, I was also being watched to see if I was truly that much better than him.

That wasn't as much of a motivator as I had hoped it would be. I didn't know if I wanted the throne, so I didn't know if I wanted to be better. I didn't want Grigick to be chosen when he was so much less competent than me, however, and as soon as I settled on that thought, I knew I had to fight through what I was feeling.

Slowly I got back to the front. By the time I did, Neritas was beginning to stumble. I leaned into him, wrapping my arm around his waist for a moment to make it look like I wanted to communicate with him secretly.

"Thank you," I whispered. "That can't have been easy."

He shook his head and gave me a quick squeeze back, then his pride kicked in and he pulled up and away from me. I let him go, appreciating the strength he was showing. It gave me some courage too. This was possible. We just had to keep walking.

It wasn't going to be so simple, though. Now that we were about halfway to the gate, I felt the growing threat of the demon, and more shadow catchers were finally beginning to arrive.

If it was difficult now, it was about to get a lot harder.

CHAPTER FOURTEEN

Leading the group along the path, I noticed the pressure lessening and everyone behind me keeping up better. Neritas, already one of the most resilient in our party, visibly straightened.

I slowed again, and Neritas noticed. More and more shadow catchers appeared in my mind. As I looked back at the group, I also saw my mother looking concerned. Her gaze met mine briefly before I looked for Alitas.

It took a few seconds longer to get his attention, but I raised my fist and shook my head, not sure how else to tell him there was a problem. Much to everyone's amazement, he jogged up the line to my side.

The whole time I kept walking slowly, and we were spread out enough that I got farther down the path, not far from a small clearing a couple of minutes away from the rotten boundary line.

"What is it?" Alitas whispered, slotting in between me and Neritas.

"Shadow catchers. Lots of them. Ahead and behind, but

more ahead." I tried not to panic, but I felt more than the last time, and as much as we had a solid group of dragons used to fighting them, we also had a group of dragons who weren't used to combat and were vulnerable.

Alitas frowned but we didn't stop moving. He took his time, thinking as we plodded on at the slowest pace I thought we could get away with. It wasn't as hard, but I suspected that was also because of the shadow catchers.

"Beginning to feel like he's setting up some sort of trap." Alitas looked at me and studied my reaction.

"I definitely don't think they're going to wait until we're almost all the way back from the gate this time," I replied.

Alitas stopped and motioned for me to do the same.

"Okay. We've got a lot of trouble ahead. We're going to have to rethink this plan," he called back.

I exhaled, relief flooding through me. Muscles that I'd barely noticed tensing relaxed. The threat of the shadow catchers in my mind was growing with each minute, and although they were holding their positions for now, that wouldn't continue. We were going to have to fight our way through them to get to the gate.

"What are we stopping for?" Capricia immediately demanded.

Everyone in the group had begun to recover a little, the pressure well and truly off mentally now. I wasn't happy about it. It might make them complacent. Brenta was soon marching up the side of the group as well, taking us out of formation.

As she made it obvious she was on the warpath, I bit my lip and concentrated on feeling the enemy. If they made a move, we were going to have to fight, and we needed as much warning as possible.

"There's a lot of shadow catchers ahead. We don't have the right group, equipment, or preparations for this many enemies. We'd be risking everyone's lives. If we could strategically draw some out and hunt them with the dragons who fight best, we can come back with everyone—"

"No, we're not turning back now." Brenta glared. "Grigick is here to sort out the gate and make it stronger. We're not turning back."

"It is not wise to proceed. But either way, it's not your call." Alitas looked at Grigick then glanced at me.

I was pretty sure he wanted me to step in and insist everyone left. Not sure what else to do, I hurried closer.

"Alitas is right. I can sense too much danger ahead. We should turn back."

"This is not what I wish," Grigick replied before Brenta could protest. "I wish to continue and show that I am as good as Scarlet is."

This didn't help, but it was exactly what I'd pushed toward.

"There are more of us than normal. Can we not fight?" Jace asked, coming up close enough that she didn't have to yell.

More of the dragons came closer as well, all of us bunching into a circle.

"It's been a little while since I've seen battle, but I can wield a weapon and hold a shield as well as the next honor guard," Elias added, and even Sarai seemed to set her jaw.

"I still wouldn't recommend it. No disrespect meant, but this is very dangerous. We might not all make it back."

"But the gate needs to be powered, does it not?" Grigick asked.

I nodded, conceding that much. He had a point.

"Then we will proceed."

Brenta and Capricia looked almost smug. Despite Grigick being the potential future king, Alitas looked at me.

How could I decide what was the right course of action? When others could die, surely I had to try to keep them alive? But I also had to weigh it against other factors. I had to protect the whole planet. And that meant making it to the gate at some point. Could we fight through?

"Are you insisting?" I asked Grigick.

He opened his mouth as if to speak but shut it again with a click. With his jaw set, he gave a single up and down of his head then looked in the direction we needed to go.

"If we must fight, we will do our best." Alitas exhaled and took charge again.

Within seconds we were back in a line and I was at the front of the group again. Alitas had shifted a few people around and a couple of the honor guards had run off into the forest for more weaponry.

Once everyone was together, we got moving again. Neritas stayed at my side.

"Be ready," I told him. "They're going to be up ahead and we should see them soon."

Although they didn't seem to be moving toward us, the shadow catchers weren't giving any ground, either. The closer we got to them, the more I felt, until I felt weighed down in a whole new way. The imposing dread made me want to flee even if no one else did.

Still, I carried on, feeling the magic of my friends and allies. Although we'd faced these monsters many times now, I still felt the same sense of dread and fear about fighting them. They could easily kill, and they weren't a foe to face lightly.

In large numbers, I didn't doubt that there would be wounded among us or that we might lose someone entirely. All this on top of having to fight the main demon's influence and heal the ground to get us to the gate. This didn't look like a walk in the park.

We were still a little way off from the very edge of the rot, but it was in sight when I noticed the first shadow catcher. Some were tracking along beside us while others had paused and were waiting out on the rotten, stinking ground ahead.

I heard some of the dragons behind me gasp and pause, I assumed because they hadn't seen the demon-controlled area before or so many of the demons. It made me feel a little better that they were taking it in and were finally as afraid as they should be, but it was too late to turn back.

"To the gate, and kill any that come too close," Capricia shouted from somewhere behind me.

I could have sworn, but instead, I reinforced my connections to everyone and all the weaponry. Before we could step out onto the rot and the first of the green dragons could join Neritas in healing the land, the two honor guards returned. They had four more with them and they all carried extra spears and had more shields slung on their backs.

They quickly distributed the extra weapons and shields and I connected to them and charged them as I had done all the others earlier in the day. It was yet more for me to have to connect to and, once again, Grigick did nothing to help.

With the group as prepared as they could be under the circumstances, I gave Neritas a nod and we moved to the edge of the area that the demon influenced. Once more, the rot had spread, and trees and pathways I had begun to get familiar with were gone, only a vague outline where some of them had once been.

I helped Neritas and borrowed a little of the magical energy from some of the stronger dragons who weren't likely to be fighting as much to help heal the land and step out toward the gate. Still, the shadow catchers didn't move, though a bunch of them paused ahead of us.

They swayed back and forth, and in the day sun they were far less corporeal, but that didn't make them any less deadly or dangerous. If anything, it made them harder to fight. Their bodies were harder to see and the edges fuzzier.

Our entire group was out on the healed land now and still moving forward. Neritas had been practicing using his powers almost every moment since he had been here last, and it showed, as he almost single-handedly grew what we needed to go forward and held it against the demon's influence.

It wasn't long after we were out in the open that the shadow catchers started to move. They flooded in, surrounding us swiftly and making it clear we were going to have to fight our way to the gate this time.

I wanted to rush forward but the ground we could stand on was limited, making this fight more challenging than any I had previously encountered.

"Want to hold ground a moment?" Neritas asked, not even looking my way.

"No. We need to keep moving or we'll definitely get trapped. Focus on giving us ground to walk into, make me space, and just block the attacks that come your way. I'll kill as many as I can."

"You got it, boss." Neritas set his jaw and I felt the magic in him flow even farther outward. Green plants sprang up across the ground in front of me, allowing me to step forward.

I readied for the first few shadow catchers, knowing I had to punch a way through for all of us and take the brunt of the force.

As the first one came within range, I slashed at its head and took it clean off. The rest of its body disappeared into a puff of smoke that clouded my vision just long enough for the next to strike at me.

Bringing the shield up, I caught the blow. Light flashed as it squealed and recoiled. As more demons joined in fights with the dragons down either side of our column, I fought hard, slashing and hacking at whatever moved ahead of me and continuing to drive forward.

At the same time, I kept connected to all the shields and swords that couldn't hold charges as Neritas' and mine could, pumping more magic into them to help protect the wielders and make their attacks more effective. It was hard to focus on so many things at once, but we were all fresh enough to the fight and I had a lot of magic to draw on.

Neritas kept the ground under my feet safe as I danced with the enemy, falling out of formation after killing the first three demons to help the dragons behind me.

"Keep trying to move forward," I told Neritas and Cios, who had been right behind me. "I'll help the weakest."

It wasn't a perfect strategy, but I was clearly more practiced. Only a couple of other shadow catchers had been killed while I had dispatched three, and my mother claimed one of those victories.

Grigick was standing in the middle of our group, eyes wide and surrounded by black dragon city guards. And this was despite me making sure that his weapon and shield were fully charged. I flew the spinning disk I had at a shadow catcher about to overwhelm one of them, hoping Neritas and Flick would also get theirs out and start using them to push the group forward and open spaces.

It hit the demon and seemed to stick inside it, zapping and cutting until it destroyed one. Then it hung there in the air and waited for me or someone else to collect it.

As our group moved toward me, my way to it blocked by more monsters and no clear path across the rot, Jace plucked it from the air. The moment she did, I charged it again.

She flicked me a grin before using it to help someone else near her. At the same time, a green dragon somewhere helped make a path in front of me so I could get to another demon that was hounding Sarai.

The older dragon had been putting up a good fight, and the monster sported some jagged edges. I struck it with my shield and sword as I rushed in from the side and delivered the final blow.

As more plumes of smoke arose around the group, hope grew in me. This was tough, but the crew was all fighting onward and we had killed enough of the monsters to make a difference.

I fought on, another demon screeching as it came at me and lunged. Its beak struck my shield, but it lashed out with its tail and caught my leg. I yelped and shifted my weight to slice its head off before it could do more damage.

My leg burned and ached where it had caught me across the calf, but I did my best to ignore it and carry on. Too many shadow catchers were nearby for me to let my guard down and check how bad it was.

In the back of my mind, I was aware of more of the monsters coming up on us, a circle of them still in the area. This felt like a trap and we were going to pay if we didn't break out of it fast.

"We need to turn back," I called, but it was so noisy that only the closest few heard me.

I'd slowly worked my way down to the middle of the group and wasn't far from Grigick when I said it, but he shook his head at me and urged everyone onward.

As the guards around him did their best to defend him, I tried to encourage him to come toward me and fight, rather than hide among them. It appeared as if he was going to refuse, but I directed some of the other guards to fight shadow catchers coming at us, organizing them more effectively and powering their weapons and shields to make them more effective.

If we stood any chance of punching through in one direction or another, we needed everyone to be on the offensive and push hard. Not sitting back and defending one dragon who should be capable of defending himself.

"Help, if you want to go forward," I yelled at him when he still cowered behind them.

This public outburst got him moving and he came closer to me. I'd have preferred him on the other side of the group and using his powers to help protect that side of it, but it was better than nothing.

As I powered up his sword and shield some more, I directed him, calling out instructions and fighting beside him. At first, he seemed to resist, but as a shadow catcher narrowly missed his body and I was forced to block the attack for him, the danger of the situation got through to him.

He gulped and started following my lead, attacking where I directed and shielding himself and those around him from errant attacks.

CHAPTER FIFTEEN

Fighting hard, I was soon panting heavily and had several more wounds on my arms and legs where tails and beaks had gotten past my defenses or I had misjudged my position. I ached and my lungs burned, but there was still magic in the group. We weren't beaten yet.

I felt the dragons growing physically tired, however, and the green dragons among us were draining faster than any of the others. The group was still making progress and we had gotten roughly halfway to the gate in the half hour we'd been fighting, but we hadn't even killed half the shadow catchers.

More kept coming, and each swipe of my blade and block from my shield depleted our power further. I was drawing from the sword and shield instead of the other dragons now, not wanting to take from them when we still had to power the gate and get back.

No sooner had I thought this than I knew we wouldn't have the power to get there and get back.

"We need to leave," I yelled again. "We can't do this.

There are too many shadow catchers and not enough of us."

Almost immediately about half the dragons with me turned to fight back the other way, no longer making the ground toward the gate green and walkable on, but trying to defend us still.

I tried to usher the rest that way, but Grigick, Brenta, and Capricia tried to resist, all of them facing the gate direction still. Brenta, despite her desires, was beholden to the dragons around her and the honor guards, and Alitas had turned with me.

"We've got to get back to safe land and figure this out another way," the captain of the honor guard said. He came in closer to Grigick and tried to appeal to him to help me guide everyone back.

At first, Grigick ignored even him, but when another shadow catcher dove toward him and hit his shield, I withdrew my magical connection and the power to keep the shield from decaying.

Although the red dragon heir had begun siphoning from others a little of the energy needed to power his weapons and armor, the dragons closest to him were running out of magic to draw on. With his skill being so new and limited, it gave him little to defend himself with.

It was a bit of a risk on my part, but I was close enough to help if necessary, and I needed him to understand that he was getting taxed and so was everyone around him. If we didn't think it was okay to keep going, it probably wasn't. I wasn't taking this decision lightly. As more of the monsters came his way and the guards around him struggled, he finally got the message.

He didn't say anything to acknowledge his agreement or try to persuade anyone else, but he allowed himself to be steered back the way we'd come and pushed in that direction with me.

With the group moving back that way, I could slink back to my place in the group, now at the back and where the worst of the enemies were concentrated.

Neritas, Flick, and Ben had been holding the position well, fighting as an effective unit and keeping us going while I went wherever I was needed most, but I rejoined them now.

Neritas was also healing the land and was clearly exhausted, and his shield was almost entirely depleted. His weapon had fared a lot worse—his fist clenched a ruin of rusted metal and decay. Despite being powered by the magic I'd pumped into everyone's weapons and shields, it seemed there were too many of them for my level of skill.

Sometimes the dragons around me needed to fight with whatever they could, charged and protected or not. In those cases, I hadn't been able to power their weapons fast enough, or with enough energy to combat the decaying effect the shadow catchers had on everything.

It was taking its toll on the group in different ways. So many were tired. I was right to call them back. I only hoped that I hadn't left it too late and that we weren't going to die out in this rotten area near the gate, unable to get to safety before we all ran out of magic.

As another shadow catcher took a blow from my shield and puffed into smoke, I had a rare moment to pause and look around me. Gaps were beginning to form here and there between the monsters we fought. The first wave was dead in large numbers, and we could have taken the shadow catchers that still fought us.

However, more and more came in from every direction. We needed to retreat faster.

I slashed and shoved, sticking to green areas and trying to defend everyone as the group turned. Although Grigick didn't want to leave and neither did the dragons with him, the rest of the group forced their hands and walked around them when they tried to go the other way.

It did my work for me, allowing me to focus on protecting everyone instead. As another monster came rushing toward me, I blocked it with the shield. The flash of light and electricity that came off it almost blinded me, but it did far more damage to the creature. I thrust at it as Neritas came back to my side and attacked as well.

Between the two of us, we cut its head off. It puffed away, giving me a little space to take stock again. I glanced over the group. My mom was out in front now and fighting hard. Jace and several others followed behind her and Reijo.

Alitas was ushering everyone along and calling orders to the other honor guards to protect all of us, but I noticed he was focusing on keeping most of them near me and Grigick. It left Elias and Sarai more exposed near the back of the retreating group, and with the monsters more concentrated there, the path behind us having been cleared of decay once already, they were struggling.

"Stay with me," I said to Neritas as I rushed back that way.

I strengthened the link between the two of us and funneled some of the magic from the stronger dragons around us into Neritas. With everything he was doing, he was draining himself fast.

So many of you weakening. It was so good of you to bring them all here to me, a familiar voice sounded in my head and made me jump.

I hesitated and almost took a beak to the stomach as I did. One of the honor guards blocked for me, overstepping and putting a foot on the rot to do so.

He gasped in pain as I pulled him back. His shoe smoked and he hopped on the other foot and yanked it off as fast as he could. Ben wrapped an arm around him and stopped him from over-balancing, and Neritas grew the grass around us so we had some more room to move. I made a mental note not to stand on rotten ground if I wanted to keep my footwear.

With one of us unable to walk properly, we couldn't carry on.

I looked at Alitas. "Get as many of them safe as you can."

He frowned, not wanting me to be left behind, but he knew I was an honor guard. It was part of my job to protect and defend, and no one could keep everyone safe as well as I could. It was important that I bring up the rear.

As Ben stooped and pulled a first aid kit from his bag to bandage the poor guy's foot, a strange noise came to my ears.

The whirring of a helicopter caught my attention again and I looked up. The news helicopters were back, but this time a national network emblem was printed on their sides. I groaned when I realized how much they could see. There were so many of us out here and so much magic was happening. Not to mention all the monsters that were strangely shimmering in this light.

I fought on, circling through the group as Ben worked on helping our temporarily downed honor guard. I still had Sarai and Elias in my group, and they were fighting on as best as they could, but the whole group was flagging.

As soon as the guard's foot was bandaged, we got moving again. Ben and Cios led the front of my group while I flitted around it wherever I was needed with Neritas almost glued to my side.

Flick gave Sarai his arm as she stumbled, taking another of my group out of the action. I felt them all getting tired as well. They had each already given me all of their energy. I might have had the most powerful dragons in two cities with me, but they weren't an endless supply of magic.

I drew more from the sword I carried, hoping to keep us all going until we could get to safety. As we finished off the few closest creatures, I noticed that the next bunch was a little way off still.

"Time to run," I called.

Thankfully, everyone listened to me this time and our group powered forward. The green dragons rallied around Neritas to grow us a path.

"I think it's easier if we follow the route the others took." Neritas looked up at the rest of the dragons who had gone ahead while we had stopped.

It wasn't clear exactly where they had gone along the whole route, but they'd left a trail where it took a while for the rot to break down the plants. It gave us somewhere to aim.

I thrust energy into everyone to give them extra strength and get them moving even faster. The gap shrunk, but we were still a couple hundred yards away from the tree line when more shadow catchers got to us. I lunged toward the closest one, almost slipping off the safe path. It was a close call and it reminded me to be careful.

Barely getting a chance to recover or think straight, I dodged an attack from another before we were surrounded again. We fought on, and my limbs grew tired.

Hearing Sarai let out a strangled squeal as a beak caught her gave me renewed energy. I fought over to her, pushing monsters out of the way with my shield in my attempts to get to her.

Flick had been helping her, but she was struggling. I pushed more power her way, but the sword was running low as well.

I glanced toward the other group. They had made it to the tree line and were safer on healthy ground. The monsters were focusing on me and my group, and the helicopter still circled overhead. It felt like it was too much to handle when I took another hit to the arm and dropped the sword.

It spun as I tried to catch it again, making it fly even farther from me. I stopped, hurting and torn between getting back to Sarai and helping her, or saving my sword.

A second later I ducked an attack and slammed my shield into yet another of the creatures. Two squealed, despite only one being hurt by me. A spear came through the first, explaining the noise before that monster poofed out of existence. I knew I couldn't take the chance of losing life over retrieving a weapon, so I turned toward the dragon who needed me.

Using my shield as a battering ram again, I thrust two more demons aside to get to the older dragon and help. Flick and I sandwiched it, and he stabbed at it while I kept it reeling off balance.

It didn't take us long. We were both well-practiced at killing these things as a team. I checked Sarai was okay, and Flick took her arm to help her keep moving. She was limping and breathing heavily, but she had a determined look on her face.

I'd seen a similar look on my mother's face in the past and I knew better than to do anything other than to help her along with whatever she was trying to do and stay out of her way. I guessed that I wore a similar expression.

Slowly, we worked our way toward the safer group. They held themselves on the grass just beyond the circle of rot and decay, fighting shadow catchers with weapons I was still charging for them. With all the practice I had been having lately and my growing skills and magic, I could still connect to all of them, although it was more taxing and I wasn't as skilled as I'd have liked over such a distance.

When we closed the gap by another hundred yards or so, with as much to go again, the weapons that had no way to store magic started to break. No matter how much I charged them, each attack on a shadow creature wore them down and rusted them until they were shadows of the former weapon. It made it harder to fight the creatures with some of us unable to attack.

The shields were holding a little better, all of them reinforced and needing a little less power, but it wouldn't be long before one of those broke as well and some of the dragons in our group became entirely defenseless. We needed to hurry and get back to the cars.

As I thought about how far we would have to fight, I despaired. The path back to the cars was narrow and long. Fighting shadow catchers while running down a narrow path was going to be difficult. The only consolation was that our green dragons wouldn't need to use magic to make a path for us once we were out of the demon's circle. I could pull on their magic instead of having to feed them the group's energy as well.

I urged everyone on again, shouting encouragement as Flick and Elias killed two more monsters and I managed to shove one onto Grigick's shield and pin it between us. Almost reflexively, he stabbed at it and finished it off.

When it puffed into smoke, I caught a smile creeping across his face. Successfully killing one of the creatures made him braver, even if I'd already done most of the work, and he whirled and stabbed at another near Alitas.

The group moved on, Neritas taking the lead again and creating more ground for us to hurry onto. We soon had another gap in waves of attacks again, and I felt more at ease in the back of my mind as both of our groups killed a few more of the demons.

Still more came.

As dragons around me ran out of magic, I hesitated. This was getting worse and I had no idea how we would make it to safety before we were overrun.

CHAPTER SIXTEEN

As Neritas connected our group to the safety of the tree line, I sighed with relief. I was out in the open, aware of the huge number of shadow catchers still alive and after us. We had to get back to the cars.

With everyone on safe land again, the green dragons became an extra arsenal in the fight, as I'd expected. I no longer needed to channel magic toward them, but could pull it out if needed. On top of that, we had momentarily managed to punch a hole in the side of the shadow catcher net and we were on the other side of the majority of them.

We had a long way to go, however, and we'd just spent a couple of hours struggling on our way out and then fighting back to the tree line. It was a long path back to the cars. Even running would take us almost half an hour. I had to get more magic from somewhere.

"Everyone pause and eat and drink something," I said. "But make it quick. We've got to run for it as soon as we can. If the shadow catchers reach us we'll need to go regardless."

I hoped that by giving everyone a small reprieve, something to fuel their bodies, and a chance for me to take stock of the magic connections and the enemies left, I could come up with enough of a plan to make everyone safe. If that didn't work, nothing would.

As everyone drank water and munched on whatever snacks could be easily pulled from bags and pockets and shared among the dragons, I closed my eyes and felt outward.

Although a lot of demons were heading toward us, we had reduced their numbers enough that the presence felt different in my mind. A lot of shadow catchers had been sent back to hell in the last two hours, but a lot remained. Their numbers made the three demons everyone had been surprised I'd survived the first time look like child's play now.

It was almost crazy to think of how far I'd come, but I opened my eyes as I felt for the familiar connections I had to the dragons ahead of me. My gaze fell on my mother first. She was charging up the weapons and shields of those around her. Two of the honor guards were using small knives to make new spears from tree branches.

Guarding the gate and facing the demons before had made them resourceful and they were helping the group, not only themselves.

In the lull, I got Neritas to go back with me and help me retrieve my sword. I instantly felt better. I would have hated to lose it, but the charge it carried had kept it safe.

As soon as I had it back firmly in my grip, I moved next to Alitas, who was issuing instructions as he passed his shield to another dragon and pulled something from his backpack.

I lifted an eyebrow at him using a frying pan but hoped the captain of the honor guard knew what he was doing.

Neritas and Flick were back by my sides, and I had powered their gear up without thinking, I was so used to doing it that the motion was now a habit. My gaze finally fell on Grigick. He was still within a small circle of city guard dragons and staring around, wide-eyed, trying to drink and eat the food Brenta encouraged his way.

Everyone else seemed to be calm and recovering, although several had injuries of various degrees. Most had already been dealt with and the ones that hadn't were minor—or on me and hadn't been noticed.

I hurt more than I wanted to focus on and I didn't dare look at the parts of me that throbbed with heat and pain. The last thing I needed was to be scared by that and distracted from keeping everyone else safe. Seeing my mother's arms and legs covered in scars from fights with these monsters had taught me that this job came with injuries and scars I would sport my entire life.

We didn't get much longer to gather ourselves before the first few shadow catchers reached us. As a group, we were ready enough for them that we made short work, outnumbering them and stabbing and slashing at them before they could do more than attack any of us.

The weapons used, except for mine, decayed a little more, but it couldn't be helped. I had to figure out what made my sword different, but now wasn't the time.

I urged everyone on again, and my mother led the way. She was an ally I hadn't known I would appreciate so much when I met her, but it gave me peace of mind to have her with me and provide the focus for everyone else.

Leaving the area was never as hard as arriving, and this time was no different. It was almost as if the demons didn't care as much now that they had achieved their objective and stopped us from getting to the gate. They still attacked, and my section of the group was the most impacted, but they didn't try to encircle us or stop us from fleeing.

After draining ourselves so much and having several more weapons break, it was a relief to be hurrying toward the cars and feel as if we could make it there without much more trouble. Not that I trusted the feeling. It was when I felt most safe that something happened and went wrong. Whatever was happening, there was a good chance I simply hadn't noticed it yet.

Either way, the best course of action was before me and I encouraged everyone to keep going. The dragons had slowed a little as they jogged along. Elias especially showed signs of struggling, and Brenta was beginning to look exhausted, although her pride had her trying to hide it.

Alitas sent more of his guards to aid them, and a lot of the hardier dragons came to the rear of the group to help me keep the demons off the back of our group. I funneled magic where it was needed, fatigue settling into my body and mind as I pushed myself harder than I had in a while.

I managed to cut the head off another monster. It puffed it into smoke as my shield drained of all the energy it had carried. This was getting dire, but we were about three-quarters of the way back to the cars and the shadow catchers were trailing out behind us, many of them dead.

Although I reached outward with my mind to gain

more magic from the other dragons, they were spent as well and I ran the risk of killing one of them if I drained more.

Slinging the shield over my shoulder and hooking it on my pack, I gave up on it. I just had to avoid getting hit. No problem.

Thankfully the nearest shadow catcher was cut down by Flick and one of the other honor guards. The two of them had worked as a pair for most of the journey so far. They had settled into a groove together.

Our group had spread out a little again, the path narrow and winding so much I could no longer see my mother, but it didn't panic me. It meant more of them were safe. All of the shadow catchers were behind us and attacking the rear of our group.

Alitas and several of the honor guards had responded to this by slipping back and fighting, but many of them were injured as well. With a few exceptions, no one's injuries needed more recovery than a few hours' rest and a stint with one of the healing devices, but I still felt guilty and angry for every single wound we'd taken.

The dragons from Detaris had assured me they knew what they were doing, and it was clear that they didn't. Grigick didn't have a clue how to use our magic and was far weaker than I was, and Brenta and Capricia had to have known this.

I pushed the thoughts away as we ran. We needed to get safe first, then I could let myself be angry. Once we were safe.

We ran on in silence for a couple more minutes. The shadow catchers were far enough behind that none of them could catch up, but the respite didn't last. Three more came screeching down the path, making enough noise that we couldn't have missed them even without my ability to sense them.

I turned at the last minute, narrowly missing being struck by a beak, and stabbed my sword deep into the side of the nearest monster. It reared up and I jumped on its tail. Neritas slid around the other side of it and hit it again, keeping it from focusing on me and letting me shift behind all three where I was safer.

Hacking and slashing where I could, I kept my distance. It took longer to finish the creatures off, and Neritas took a small gash to one arm and Alitas lost his makeshift shield to decay when the frying pan rusted through, but eventually, the three demons were dealt with.

Our group rushed onward, almost sprinting to catch up with the dragons who had continued fleeing. It was an effective strategy, giving the slower dragons time to make headway before we caught up to them again and protected their flight.

This time, when we reached the back of the slowest group, I could sense no more shadow catchers running after us, and we could just about see the parking lot ahead. It emboldened everyone and gave them enough hope to push through the pain and tiredness to go the last hundred yards or so.

Despite the relative safety, I stayed at the back of the group and made sure everyone else got to the cars ahead of me. Some got in the cars immediately, like Sarai, who was so tired she needed help just to lift her legs into the car.

I felt sorry for her, but before I could think much about

it an argument broke out among the dragons in the middle of the parking lot.

Brenta and Capricia were standing with Grigick on one side of the group, and my mother, Ben, and Reijo were on the other. More dragons joined them, city guards gravitating to the former side while Jace and Cios moved to the other. I headed toward the middle, sure of only one thing right now: an argument on the doorstep of an enemy who had already drained us was a really bad idea.

"You all wanted this to fail from the beginning so it would make Grigick look incompetent," Capricia said when I came in earshot.

"No, Grigick looked incompetent all on his own," Jace returned, as casually as if she were stating the most boring of facts. A couple of the others snorted laughter, but this only made Capricia and Brenta angrier, and Grigick's cheeks flushed.

"There were too many shadow catchers," I said before anyone else could explode. "No matter who was leading the group, we'd have had to turn around and make a new plan. It's not Grigick's fault and it's not anyone else's. I'd have turned around sooner and tried a different strategy rather than using our energy the way we did, but we sent a lot of those demons back where they came from. That's a sort of victory."

This seemed to calm the situation a little, but everyone was still on edge. And we still needed to decide what to do next.

"Our mission should never have been attempted. And I was set against it from the beginning." Capricia crossed her arms in her usual aggressive stance, and I fought not to roll my eyes. "We should go back to Detaris, crown Grigick, and forget this madness.

"Scarlet saved us, and she already told you this was necessary. I'm not bowing to a red dragon who cowered and did nothing while she powered all our weapons and worked with her mother and the honor guards to keep us alive," Jace insisted.

More dragons nodded in agreement than I'd expected, including some of the city guards. This angered Capricia further.

"You didn't give him a chance to help, taking all the glory for yourself," Brenta snapped.

I felt my temper flaring and bit down on my desire to tell her I gave him every chance and it wasn't my fault he was a pathetic excuse for a red dragon. It was no easy task.

"If we had been left in Grigick's care, none of us would have survived," one of the other honor guards said. His spear was rotten and almost useless from how many times he had shoved it into shadow catchers. "Not once did he harness the magic the way Scarlet did to aid us in fighting."

"Do you even know how, Grigick?" Cios asked, his tone gentle as he addressed the dragon directly.

"I do," Grigick claimed. "But this is the first time I have fought shadow catchers at all, let alone an entire group. I don't have the experience Scarlet does, but that doesn't mean I am incapable. I am sure my powers can grow as hers have if I am given the chance to prove I am worthy. We could kill all of these monsters."

I frowned as Grigick tried to be passionate and win back the dragons around him. Although I had no idea if it swayed anyone, I couldn't decide if I respected him for not giving up or thought him a fool for not understanding that he would never have what it took. The second I had realized I could funnel magic and use my powers to harm shadow catchers, I experimented and made it work. No one had taught me anything.

"We should rest and go back as soon as we can. I will show you all that I just need to learn and practice and that I'm just as powerful as Scarlet." Grigick looked around as if desperate for someone to agree with him.

"You aren't as powerful as Scarlet. Doesn't take a genius to see that. Even if it's a matter of training," Sarai called from the nearby car, where she'd had her injuries seen to. She hobbled back over to us while leaning on a cane.

Although I admired her ability to push through discomfort, none of this helped. If our group splintered, we wouldn't achieve anything. While I had us all working together, we had a chance to beat the demon and power up the gate again, but I needed calm tempers to help come up with a new plan.

"Scarlet has been blessed by the ancestors," my mother reminded everyone. "She went to Kilnar and stood before them. She's more powerful because she's proven herself and earned their blessing."

A silence followed this proclamation. Most knew that was the case, but not everyone did, and it wasn't easy to argue with. I noticed Grigick appeared more unsettled by this than anything so far. Capricia and Brenta took it in stride, having heard it before. They were equally as unimpressed as they had been the first time, but the reaction of the group gave them pause.

As I studied them and tried to work out what they were thinking, the pair studied everyone else.

"We could solve all this really easily. Go before the ancestors as well, Grigick. If they give you their blessing as well, you will definitely have the power needed to match Scarlet with the training and we can then try this again with all of us as strong as we can be." My mother didn't look at me, but directly at Grigick, almost challenging him.

Grigick gulped. "Then this I will do."

Capricia and Brenta gasped. I froze. This was going to be an interesting turn of events. Would the ancestors bless two of us at once? There was only one way to find out.

CHAPTER SEVENTEEN

Before anyone could come up with a plan or discuss Mom's suggestion, the sound of a helicopter came closer and cars on the road began heading toward us.

"I think we should take this somewhere more private," Alitas said. "We're drawing a lot of human interest lately and we need to make sure they don't come here and get themselves in trouble."

"There's also a lot of shadow catchers nearby," I added, noticing that while we had been arguing they had crept closer, even if they weren't full-out charging us.

We had cars, which would make it difficult for them to stop us from leaving, but if they circled us it could still cause a problem.

"We'll go to the farmhouse Elias and Sarai own," Alitas proposed before anyone else could suggest going back to Detaris or somewhere else.

I'd thought of the yacht, but it wasn't big enough for a group this large. Sarai and Elias nodded and said they'd lead the way, and even Grigick moved toward his car before Capricia and Brenta could complain.

So many dragons hurried off that the pair had no choice but to comply or be left behind. It was a relief to get back into a car with Neritas, Flick, Alitas, and Ben and be out of danger and view again for a while. The pressure was getting to me and I needed a moment away from it to think, rest, and recover.

As soon as we were on the road again, Flick pulled some food from his bag and handed it out between us. I was grateful and settled down to munch. I also finally looked at the wounds on my body.

Neritas gasped as he saw how hurt I was. I had a deep gash across one calf, and a shallower one on my arm. They were beginning to heal, my mind having automatically funneled the magic into the process, but I reached into my pack and pulled out one of the healing devices I had with me anyway.

Although I had drained a lot of my magic already, it never took long for me to feel as if I had something in reserve again, and healing was an energy-efficient task with these handy little devices, so I soon got to work. It quickly took the pain away, making the wounds itch as I sped up my body's natural healing process.

It wasn't a miracle. My mom had explained it as using the stores the body has available and speeding up a natural process, which was why it could only do so much before the body needed a break and it could be used again.

As soon as I healed enough to not hurt and the itching had subsided, I stopped. It didn't use much magic, but I didn't want to use any more than I had to.

With my basic needs taken care of, my friends and I discussed what had happened. If it hadn't been for the dragons in my car, far more people would have been hurt, and some would have died. As it was, none of us had life-threatening injuries.

We hadn't achieved much more than dispatching a bunch of demons, however. Not really.

"It achieved more than that," Neritas protested when I voiced what I was thinking. "It showed a bunch of dragons that despite Grigick's support from Brenta and Capricia, he's not as competent as you, and he's a coward on top of that."

Although Neritas had a point, I wondered how it had helped me. Most of the dragons with us were willing to support me anyway, either because Alitas did and they answered to him, or because they'd already seen me fight the shadow catchers.

I wasn't sure what the rest thought. Because we'd needed to clear the parking lot before we were pinned down by more shadow catchers and nosey humans, I hadn't had time to talk to Griffin or Liam and Hiachi. They weren't used to this sort of thing and might have been terrified themselves.

Hiachi had been injured as well, and the honor guards near Griffin had saved him from being gored by a shadow catcher's beak. Although they had been positive toward me before arriving at the gate, people reacted differently to finding themselves in danger. Capricia had blamed me though I'd fought alongside her in the past, and others might feel similar.

I had to go with Grigick to the island. If the ancestors

had blessed me and given me their powers, I must have a part to play, as queen or as something else. On top of that, I needed to know for sure if they blessed Grigick, and I didn't trust him not to lie.

I spent the rest of the journey talking to Alitas about what the honor guard would do in this situation. Would they help protect Grigick? Would they go all the way to the sacred area?

"I've been there a couple of times with your father and mother," Alitas replied. "Although I wasn't given the honor of being taught how to get there, and I'm not sure I could have sensed the path as your father taught your mother to, I was trusted with the journey and seeing the most holy area a couple of times. Your father sought advice there more than once."

This was all the convincing I needed. My mind was made up. I was going to go there, with Grigick or not.

After all the conversations, eating, and healing, we arrived at our destination and I could get out of the car and stretch my legs. I was emboldened by the familiar sight. I had found refuge here in the past and I was grateful to be back again.

Brenta looked around at the working farm in disgust, her nose wrinkling at the smell of animals and their feces. Although I wasn't used to it, something about it seemed natural to me, and I didn't mind. People had to eat, and the animals had to be looked after somewhere.

"You're all welcome inside," Sarai said, her usual temper forgotten as she slipped into host mode. "Please, come and rest and recover from today's ordeals. We have beds enough for everyone among the cottages and main house, and there is always plenty of food."

Walking toward the farmhouse, I realized Sarai and Elias must have been planning for something like this for some time. They had been running an information organization that had been looking for me and had supported me entirely since the moment I had proven who I was. All their efforts on top of that had been put into fighting demons and helping me fix the gate.

Unlike previous occasions I had been here, there weren't a lot of dragons lingering in the kitchens. A few were bustling around the kitchen as they finished making a very large meal.

"The biggun's up," one of them called to Sarai as she came into the kitchen after me.

I glanced back at her, and she nodded as if this was exactly what she expected. Not wanting to get in the way of people who had a job to do, I stepped to one side of the kitchen and let Sarai and the chefs move freely without me blocking their paths.

"There's room for all to dine out this way," the elder said, leading the way for the group that had begun building in the dining section of the kitchen.

Sarai walked down the length of the large table and out through another door that led into a courtyard behind the farmhouse. Where there had been an open area of flagstone beauty before, a large white tent covered the expanse, hooked to the buildings on either side and providing shelter from the elements.

Most of the dragons I usually saw at the farmhouse were

out there, moving large tables around to get the best layout for so many people. It looked almost like a wedding reception as they worked to make it look decent and give everyone space.

"We can eat out here, talk as we wish, and retire when we're done." Sarai motioned for some people to sit down and others to help set everything up.

Wanting to set a good example, I moved to a stack of chairs and handed a couple to Neritas, then handed a couple to Flick. We quickly laid them out, doing the work for those who couldn't or were otherwise engaged. I saw my mom and some of the more severely injured dragons head to the plates and a large stack of tablecloths. Within seconds Mom was coordinating them being laid out as well.

With so many willing and eager to help, we soon had the area finished and ready for people to eat, just in time for the kitchen staff to call for help and the dishes to start coming our way.

Soon the tent was full of the heavenly aroma of food and we were all sitting down to eat. With any luck, full bellies and some time to rest would improve everyone's mood and we would be able to plan the future in a more civilized manner.

Before I had finished eating, so famished I added a third helping to my plate, Grigick, Brenta, Capricia, and several of the guards from the city came over to our table.

Alitas had some of the honor guards move, and Griffin and Reijo gave up their seats so we could talk. Anxiety made my throat tighten, but I fought to appear relaxed on the outside. This conversation was necessary, and it was a good sign that they had come to me.

"I need your mother to guide me to the island of the ancestors," Grigick said. "The knowledge of it wasn't passed down my line of dragons."

"That is a sad event, but we will definitely accompany you to the island." I beckoned my mother, who had been sitting farther away and hadn't heard herself being mentioned.

"No, we wish to go with a small group—just a few guards from the city—and have your mother direct us."

I burst out laughing, thinking of the difficulties of getting a boat to the island, how it required specific knowledge and conditions, and how I'd never have gotten there if my mother hadn't led me the whole way.

"You're not going anywhere without the honor guard and without someone to guide you the whole way. Even if I thought you could do it alone, I would insist that some of us are coming with you. It's not very simple to get to, and that's an understatement. I couldn't guide you, and that's with having been there once."

Brenta shook her head and looked pointedly at Grigick. He exhaled and turned his attention to me.

"My daughter is right," Mom said as she joined us. "We're all going with you, or you can find the place on your own. I couldn't direct you well enough without you getting yourselves killed along the way. And we'll need your parents or guardians for this to work."

Grigick's eyes went wide and he gulped again, looking at Capricia this time. Although she tried to be subtle, she shook her head just a fraction.

"That won't be possible," Grigick insisted.

"Then you will need two dragons who can take their

places and speak of your honor. They'll—"

"We can do it," Brenta interrupted.

My mother shrugged as if it wasn't worth the argument.

"But we really must insist that we go alone."

"I'm going. I wish to go back to the ancients myself. And it's not negotiable." I folded my arms across my chest, knowing I had the upper hand and they couldn't do anything about it. Making Brenta fume was an added benefit.

"You would withhold this from him yet claim you're treating him fairly and giving him the opportunity to prove he can lead." Brenta grew more shrill as she didn't get her way and no one else seemed to care.

"I'm not withholding anything from him. He can go. But alone you will both get yourselves killed and I won't get the confirmation I need that the ancestors give their approval either way. It is not just me who has to be appeased for this to work." I wasn't sure my words were true, and I was grateful I wasn't in the elders' chambers in Detaris. They were stuck doing this our way or they could slink back to Detaris with even less support than they'd left with. Grigick had no choice, and he knew it.

"We'll do this your way if we must. But I do it under protest and I will insist on approaching the ancestors first, to be sure they haven't been biased against me before I talk to them."

"I couldn't care less what order we do it in. I have no intention of making this unfair. I'm even willing to help you as much as I can, despite what Brenta and Capricia think of me. But if we are going, there is no sense in sitting around here any longer. It is important that we go at the right time."

I got to my feet. It would take some coordination with Alitas and the others to organize the trip. We'd stay out there overnight and I wanted to make sure we had better provisions than we had the last time.

Thankfully, Elias and Sarai had already started organizing everything based on Jace's account of the previous journey, proving yet again that they were prepared to be involved in all sorts of elements of my life. This time the elderly dragons were staying behind to heal and continue to look for strategies and technology to fight the demon behind the gate and increase our chances of getting it powered up.

Knowing a technology existed that could be used to help had increased interest in finding more of it. I suspected Detaris had more, and a little more remained in the cache I'd found near the gate, but I didn't want to use our energy to get more of that yet. Not when I could be turning it over to someone who could one day use it against me.

Thankfully, they had never asked where it had come from or expected me to provide any. It was clear to them it was limited as we only had a few items of each type. And I felt guilty for not picking up the rest, but it had taken a lot out of me, and I didn't have the strength now to get the rest.

Within an hour we were ready to leave again, a slightly smaller group but more prepared and better equipped. It was time to see if the ancestors approved of Grigick, even if I wasn't sure of my path one way or another.

CHAPTER EIGHTEEN

I settled into the car at the head of our convoy again. It was beginning to feel familiar and almost comforting for its regularity. In the last few minutes, as we were getting everyone organized to leave, Mom and I felt the far-off presence of more demons. I wasn't sure if they were doing much, other than keeping an eye on us, but I'd warned everyone staying at the farmhouse anyway and urged everyone else to hurry.

"Drive slower than usual for a mile or two." I made sure Ben understood that I wanted the shadow catchers to know we had left. So far, they had never attacked anywhere I wasn't, so I wanted to give them the chance to notice I was leaving and wouldn't be back. It gave Sarai and Elias as much safety as I could provide them right now.

Alitas wasn't happy about it, but a single glance seemed to satisfy him that I wasn't going to be argued with on this one. It only increased the risk to us a little. The creatures couldn't reach the island, so we'd be safe once we were there. I didn't doubt that the most sacred location for our kind was in the middle of a large lake because of this.

The drive was quiet as I thought about what I would ask the ancestors if I could. I needed help. If Grigick was the better choice of the two of us, I would happily stand aside, but he wasn't looking like it currently. But did I really want to face the dragons in Detaris again and demand I be crowned their queen?

Even thinking about living in the city again made me feel sick. It had been a toxic atmosphere. There were other options. It was clear that other cities would happily accommodate me if I wanted to be queen and rule from their locations. But that could lead to one or more cities refusing to recognize my reign.

Whatever I did had possible risks, and that was why I wanted to seek counsel. I needed to know if I was missing something, or if the ancestors had faced similar issues in the past. Did any of it matter if the gate wasn't protected?

Darkness surrounded us before we got to the shore of the lake and the familiar sight of several boats waiting for us, exactly the right number again, five this time instead of three. Reijo, Ben, and Cios took up positions to steer three of them. My mother guided Reijo in his.

Guessing that Capricia would try to nab the last one, I moved toward it before she could. She was only a step behind me and she glared at me as I stepped into position. The way the dock was lit up gave her expression an even more sinister edge.

"Out of the way, Red. I'm going to protect Grigick."

"Fantastic. Then you can sit beside him in the middle of this boat and allow me to concentrate on just navigating us through what's ahead. After all, you know how difficult that is to get through, don't you?" I smiled at Capricia and sat.

Sometimes I wondered why she continued to challenge me on my decisions. So far I hadn't backed down on anything when it came to her, and I didn't plan to let her have her way any time soon. There was a lot about her I didn't understand, however, and I was going to have to accept it as yet another confusing element.

I thought she might argue with me, but it appeared that she was getting as tired of our confrontations as I was. She did as I suggested, although she also made sure Brenta was safe in the boat with us. Neritas and Flick once more refused to be separated from me, and with Grigick and Griffin joining us, we were almost full.

Another honor guard joined us to fill our boat, and we waited for the rest of the dragons to get seated and allow us to leave. One boat ended up being purely city guards and honor guards, but it made little difference what order we were in.

Now that I was close to the island again, I felt my connection to it like a thin thread in my mind. Concentrating on it made it more obvious and thicker, but I also noticed shadow catchers in the far reaches of my mind. They appeared to be ignoring us, as coming for us would have done no good.

As we pushed off the dock and got ourselves moving, I wondered if I had managed to stretch my capacity enough finally to detect them before they could detect me, but I had no way of testing it or knowing for sure yet. Either way, they didn't try to follow, and they slipped from my mind, taking the unease their presence gave me with them.

With the connection to the ancestors I'd gained the last time I was here, I could have navigated toward the island, even in the dark and thick fog as last time. I suspected an unknown magic had created the fog before, perhaps to deter others from coming in this direction, but it could have been a coincidence.

It was soon difficult to see anything but the boat in front and occasionally the boat in front of them. We had ropes between us, as we had the first time, to ensure no boat got left behind.

None of this scared me as it had the first time. Going closer to the island gave me a feeling similar to but entirely opposite from the shadow catchers. A peace and safety that came from being in a loving home. At least, that was what I hoped a loving home would feel like. The only place I had felt similar had been Anthony's apartment. I had begun to feel relief in Ben's home in Detaris, but never as relaxed as I did with Anthony.

This island had a draw to it, however, that let me know I was going somewhere safe and welcoming.

As we continued, I got the impression that the feeling was mine alone. Everyone else shifted in, toward the center of the boat, staring around them in the dark, and the honor guard's grip on the rope of the boat in front grew tighter. I considered reassuring them, but the part of me still pissed off at Brenta and Capricia kept me silent.

Seeing Grigick look around him with wide eyes and feeling the heavy silence over the boat as they endured the gloom was almost satisfying. This was yet another unknown to him. As the rocks started to appear around us, I made our boat a source of light, using my innate dragon ability to make them easier for us to see.

Flick shifted in the boat to call out rocks on our port side, the honor guard let me know what lay ahead, and Neritas leaned to the starboard side. Between them they helped guide me, making sure I didn't hit the many sharp-looking stones as we followed the boat in front. The atmosphere grew tenser as the warnings kept coming and we had to slow to make sure we made it through safely.

Time slipped by, but I didn't falter. The warnings helped but a strange peace helped me find the path as well. It was as if the correct movements came to my hands anyway, now and then my body moving to avoid a rock as it was spotted by one of the dragons with me.

The boats between my mother's at the front and mine in the middle struggled and soon bunched up, forcing me to go slower. After frowning for a moment, I made all of their boats glow a little and hoped the increased light would make the dangers easier to spot so they could react a little faster.

It helped, but our progress was still slower than on the first trip we had made, and by the time we were in safer waters I was exhausted by the need to keep my powers active. On top of the fighting earlier in the day and focusing on sensing the demons ever since, I was low on energy.

We pulled the boats ashore as soon as everyone was out and on dry land, and the group naturally split into three: those who were from Detaris and still supported Grigick, those from Detaris and the other cities who supported me or were civilians, and my family, close friends, and the honor guard.

The middle group was the smallest, but that it existed at all was something to be pleased with, and as soon as I realized it had formed I moved closer to them.

"I know many of you are tired. If you wish to rest, we can set up some tents here for you. There is no great need for you to go any further tonight." I smiled at them and pointed to a clearing nearby that could just be seen in the dark.

"If it's all the same to you, I'd like to go as far as the ancestors allow." Griffin looked around himself as if this was a grand adventure and he was in paradise already. "It's not every day a dragon gets to stand on the island of the ancestors."

The majority of the group shared the sentiment, and those who weren't as enthusiastic were at least willing to continue, which settled the matter entirely. All of us were continuing. Again, I felt my body reacting as if I instinctively knew the way, guiding me toward the right path before my mother could even move.

A grin slid across her face and she motioned for me to take the lead. Although I should be giving Grigick a chance to lead and not acting as if I was in charge, it felt right to be taking everyone somewhere I had been, where I felt at home. If Brenta and Capricia didn't like it, I was far enough away from them that I couldn't see their faces in the dark.

With all of us safe on the island, no one needed to feel as if they were on guard duty or to take up any particular order. Everyone milled about and talked to whomever they wished. I soon found the diplomatic types from every group were sticking closer to me, so I slowed my pace and chose the wider paths to accommodate them.

To my surprise, Capricia joined us, and for the first time in a while, she didn't glare at me the second our eyes met.

"How many times have you been here before?" Hiachi asked me. The trees around us showed many paths but my feet didn't falter to take us toward the middle of the island.

"Just once," I replied as I took a left turn without really thinking about it. It appeared to turn back the way we'd come, but it was soon veering right again, around a large rock and a thicket of bushes and other trees I wouldn't have wanted to tangle with.

"But you know the way without hesitation?" Griffin asked.

"Yes. I think so. I didn't the first time, but since connecting to the ancestors it's as if there is a trail to follow. Like a thread that my mind can feel but my eyes can't see."

"This is how it is for all red dragons the ancestors have blessed." My mom's voice rang loud and clear in the night from where she lingered near the back of the group. She was the comforting presence that helped me know I was making the right choices. I had no doubt that she would warn me if I took a wrong turn, but so far she had said nothing.

Hiachi, Griffin, and even Capricia looked around at the next few joining paths and turn-offs as if they hoped to see or feel the trail as well, but their awe only grew as I led them onward and around many obstacles, from deep ponds to sudden crevices, small bog-like areas, and even groups of animals.

A few times, the path grew narrow and Neritas and another couple of the green dragons encouraged the plants to grow away from us, using their magic to widen the path and make our passing as a group easier.

"It is almost as hard as the gate area is to persuade to grow another way," Neritas whispered to me when we reached the third bottleneck. "And I think it goes back when our minds let go of the plants again."

I nodded, taking in the information. It was an interesting theory and was probably right. It made sense that this island was kept the way it was with magic. It made me wonder what powered it. Did it also need charging like the pillars at the gate?

If it did, it was important to know. I wanted to know how that worked, so I made a mental note to look for the information as soon as I got the chance. Everything we learned could potentially help us save our race and even the entire world.

Neritas slipped away from me a moment later. I glanced back to see him waiting by a particularly narrow section of the path. His eyes were closed and I knew he would be feeling outward with his mind, trying to figure out what was going on. I left him to it. He would catch up when he was ready.

"The ancestors really didn't want just any dragon to find them, did they?" Hiachi asked when I confidently took another turn that appeared as if it would go wrong.

"The ancestors wanted only the strongest heirs to ever be able to find the heart of our kingdom," my mother's voice came from behind us. I hadn't noticed her approach. "It is a closely guarded secret, and if it wasn't for the great need we find ourselves in to establish an heir and to power the gate before the great demon is released once more, none of you would even be here." My mother didn't look at any of them as she spoke but continued to walk, her head tilted up as if she saw something ahead that none of the rest of us could.

As I looked in the direction she did, I felt a tug, a pull toward something above and beyond our view that had begun so gradually I hadn't noticed it before now. It grew as we continued, giving urgency to my steps.

"We might need to take a break," Griffin said a few minutes later.

I noticed he was panting and others around me were out of breath. My own heart was racing, and I realized I had accidentally picked up the pace.

"Sorry," I replied, stopping to let everyone catch up and rest. "We're close now."

Just a long climb up to the plateau and the final winding pathway to the shrine itself. Given how long it had taken to get this far, I didn't expect to get to the shrine for a few more hours, and it made me wonder if we'd get any sleep tonight. I had been better rested the last time I had been here and had a more able group with me. This was...different.

CHAPTER NINETEEN

When we reached the steeper climb up the next part of the island mountain, I heard several of my companions groan.

"Anyone who doesn't wish to go on can rest here," I offered, lifting my voice enough that they could all hear me. Some of them looked at each other, but no one opted to stay. They had come this far.

Without another word, I began the climb, but I took pity on the weakest. I pulled a little magic from the strongest of us and fed it into all the dragons who visibly struggled with the climb, including Brenta. She looked up and around as I did it, feeling it but not sure where it came from.

"Was that you?" I heard her ask Grigick.

A bend in the path above allowed me to see them easily. He hesitated in his reply and looked confused enough by the question that he answered it without speaking. A fraction of a second later Brenta looked up at me. I gave her a small nod, confirming it had been me.

Whatever had been said and happened between us, I didn't want a journey this special to be overshadowed by pain and exhaustion for any of us. And maybe Brenta would understand me a little more if I helped her when she most needed it. Whatever anyone had done in the past, I wouldn't let them suffer needlessly. It just wasn't in my nature.

We had to pause several more times on the way up. Natural alcoves and larger flat areas were built into the path to accommodate stops here and there, although few of them were large enough for the whole group. It soon became apparent that it was going to take too long for everyone to get up to the top. Night was slipping away, and my mother's face showed concern.

"We're going to have to leave some of them to come up in their own time," she whispered to me when the weaker ones asked to stop again. "They'll be safe enough at this point."

I looked back at them, feeling how drained many of them were, and nodded. She had a point. We needed to get to the top, and there was another path after this one that only some of us could take. But it wasn't going to go down well.

"I'll stay with the others and bring them up later." Alitas had noticed us talking. "Take whoever you need on with you. I've been here enough times before that I know the way."

It was a relief to hear his offer and I immediately took him up on it. I encouraged Grigick to join me, along with the two people who were there to support him. Of course,

Brenta was one of those, and it didn't help the problem much to have to bring her too. She was one of the dragons struggling.

Neritas offered her his arm and Flick moved to support her as well. Neither of them had featured in my plans to take any further than the plateau most had camped on the last time, but I wasn't going to be able to leave them behind this time.

We carried on—Ben, Reijo, my mother, Neritas, Flick, Capricia, Brenta, and Grigick—while everyone else stuck with Alitas and the other honor guards. Pushing the guilt and the pain in my body away, I carried on walking and funneling magic to Brenta to help her carry on. With Neritas and Flick helping her she managed to move faster, but it still took another half an hour to get to the plateau.

"This is where most of the dragons will stop and wait for us," Reijo explained as he sat by the bottom of the next section of the path. "I'll make sure they know not to come any higher."

Just as before, the bushes that led this way seemed to light up at our presence if I or my mother came closer to them. I got the impression they weren't lighting up for Grigick, but it was hard to tell when we were still mostly moving as a group. All of us were tired now, but we couldn't stop. We needed to go the rest of the way, and I felt the tug pulling me onward.

I couldn't talk. My mind was only able to support Brenta with our magic and focus on moving. The day had been long and exhausting and I wasn't finished yet. Now and then I glanced back, seeing the glowing plant life fade into darkness again after we passed. Something was beautiful about it as it led us closer to the island's inner sanctum.

The pillars came into view and relief washed through me. It gave strength to my weary limbs and helped me climb the last part. My mother wasn't far behind, followed by Grigick with Ben.

I heard the red dragon gasp and look around at the pillars and patterns on the floor. All of it was aglow, faint lines lighting everything like some magical wonderland. The tug in my stomach finally faded away, and my entire body relaxed for the first time in several hours.

Something about this place felt safe, like returning home at the end of a difficult and trying day. I was welcome here, and known.

"This is the temple of our ancestors?" Grigick moved toward the middle.

"It is, but you should be careful where you step and what you touch until you and those with you are ready." My mother moved toward the circle she had stood in when I had communed with the ancestors, and Ben moved naturally toward the other.

Wondering whether this would work, but feeling strangely calm either way, I encouraged Grigick to come over to me.

"Brenta, go stand with Ben." My mother pointed at my mentor. Neritas escorted her around the raised center, making sure not to stand on anything himself.

Although I hadn't explained much about this place to my friends, Flick also gave everything a wide berth and pointed out the route my mother had taken to Capricia. She followed it, sensible enough to also be careful, and Mother and Ben helped their counterparts get into place while I told Grigick where to stand and what to do.

"It shouldn't hurt and shouldn't take long," I said once he was in place before I hurried out of the area as well. Ben stayed with Brenta, the tired elder looking as if she would collapse at any moment.

My mother shifted back around the edge of the area to join me, Neritas, and Flick to wait and watch. Once everyone was in position, Brenta and Capricia stepped forward and Grigick put his hands on the dais.

Nothing happened.

I raised an eyebrow as the three of them looked at each other and then at us. No one spoke as the three of them stepped out of their circles and back into them, repeating the lead-up that should have triggered the ancestral temple and sought their approval as it had for me.

Still, nothing happened.

"How do you get this to work?" Grigick asked me, looking back over his shoulder. I shrugged. If it wasn't working for them, I had no idea why.

"The ancestors would have connected to you already if they wished to," my mother replied. This earned her a glare from Brenta.

Grigick turned back and tried for a third time, but it was as fruitless as the first two times. The three of them hesitated and fidgeted, but none of us moved to help or deter them from trying as many times as they wished.

"Show us how it works for you," Capricia demanded.

Her tone was more menacing than I'd have expected given the situation we were in.

I considered her words. She didn't wait but walked my way around the edge of the area. Ben looked at me as well, as if he was waiting for me to decide if we should allow them to see it.

"Are you sure you want me to approach the ancestors before you?" I asked Grigick, hoping he was calm enough to think this through.

"Show us again what to do, but don't do it yourself." He stepped to the side, giving me the space I would need to stand in his place.

"Okay, I'll try to get as close to doing it as I can without actually doing it, but there's not much to it." I moved back toward him as my mother and Ben returned to the other two circles. It was even easier for them. They simply stood in the right place and the magic happened for them.

I got the impression that it was Grigick who was stopping this from working for Brenta and Capricia. He hadn't known how to channel our magic or how to use most of his red dragon abilities, and the island wasn't responding to him in the same way it was me.

I kept this thought to myself. I walked back to the pedestal and the circle it stood in and showed Grigick every tiny detail from where I put my feet to where I intended to place my hands and even where I looked.

"Then you just connect to it." He looked at me as if he had done exactly that. "Using your magic," I added in a half-whisper.

He narrowed his eyes as if he didn't understand why I had added this, so I stepped back and away once more, hoping he understood me this time. The entire time we had been traveling, I hadn't considered that Grigick might not be able to get the dais to work and wouldn't even get the chance to show the ancestors he existed.

My mind had run through different scenarios of what might happen instead. The ancestors might smite him for daring to disturb them without actually being worthy to do so. Or perhaps for lying about his parentage, something I was fairly sure he had done. At least one of them was still alive. But one of them was also not pure red—of that I was certain.

On the opposite end of my thoughts, I had considered what might happen if the ancestors connected to him and found that his heart was more pure than mine. Would they take the extra power they had given me and hand it to Grigick instead? Was that a price I might have to pay because I had brought him here?

While I thought over these scenarios and wondered how likely any of them might be now, Grigick tried once more, and my mother and Ben got out of the way of their counterparts again. Despite what I had told Grigick, nothing happened, and I heard a growl from Capricia as she shook her head. Even Brenta started to turn her ire on the male dragon in the center of us all.

"I'm sorry, Grigick. I do not think the ancestors wish to bless you." My mother's voice was quiet and gentle. I appreciated her tact and her attempt at not making too big a deal of it, but he whirled, anger blazing in his eyes. Ben moved closer to him as Neritas' hand moved to rest on the hilt of his sword.

My mother ushered them away from her as if she were perfectly safe.

"I think you still have some soul-searching to do and perhaps some more learning and practice are needed before you can get the ancestors to connect to you and listen, but if you ever wish to return, you have my word that I will guide you again. The knowledge of this place and how to use it should not rest in so few hands. It was once a secret all red dragons guarded and a place precious to many."

"Thank you," Grigick replied as he came closer to us. He sounded different, as if it pained him to speak, and his gaze remained turned down.

Wondering if he was fighting back tears and not wanting to make him feel as if he was being too emotional in a spotlight, I deliberately focused my attention on the other dragons.

"Do you wish to witness me connecting with the ancestors to see that it can be done?" I walked to the dais and waited for Capricia and Brenta to reply before I put my hands on it or tried to mentally connect to it one way or another. I wasn't going to do it yet, not until I had some idea of who was going to be where.

"We don't need your bragging," Capricia replied as she strode off. She grabbed Grigick's arm, and I got the impression that the guy was in a lot of trouble. This hadn't gone the way they'd planned.

Stomping and huffing and clearly in a bad mood, she pulled him back down the pathway. The bushes didn't light up for them as they had for me on the way up or down last time, and this made the city guard captain growl even more. Brenta followed, pulling out a flashlight and at least making herself useful to the trio.

Although I felt bad for Grigick that it hadn't worked, it solidified what I needed to do in my head. If he wasn't capable of being blessed by the ancestors, I would take charge whether I wanted to or not. The gate needed defending and I was the only dragon who could do it. In some ways, it answered my questions and made me wonder if I should bother the ancestors myself.

But something drew me to the dais in the center once more.

"You don't need us to connect this time. Not now the ancestors have opened to you," Mom explained before I could put my hands on it again. "We will leave you to consult them. Come down to us when you're ready."

I nodded toward her and waited as everyone filed away. Neritas looked as if he was going to object, but Ben was behind him and motioned for him to follow and leave. He checked that I was okay, and the look was enough for me to see the concern and the offer to stick with me, but it seemed right to do this alone, and I preferred the idea of him being down with the others, protecting my interests while I was absent.

Although Neritas might not have realized it yet, it looked like he was going to get what he wanted. I had to step into the role of queen and force the hands of the people around me. But that was where I was most scared. I didn't want to divide an already fractured group.

Even though everyone had gone and the glow was

fading into the background as my mother lit the plants that led the way back down, I hesitated. What if the ancestors didn't like me coming back to them? What if they were just as reluctant to talk to me as they had been to Grigick?

At least I would have no witnesses to my failure, I thought.

CHAPTER TWENTY

I considered walking away from the dais and not even approaching the ancestors, not sure my ego could handle the rejection that Grigick had just suffered, but the tug in the pit of my stomach to go toward it returned if I even took a single step toward the path. Something in me or from them wanted me to connect, and it gave me the confidence to try.

Putting my hands on the dais did nothing, but I closed my eyes and reached for the magic in it with my mind. It reached for me even more eagerly and connected to me. The tug came back, but the sensation was far more pleasant and lasted only a moment. Within a fraction of a second, I felt the warmth of another mind. One that felt deeply for me.

Although I was still standing at the dais with my eyes closed and my hands resting on it, it was also as if I was in another place, my eyes opening to see a familiar room in Detaris. The royal tower where I had lived briefly. The decor was a little different, but it was unmistakable. I could even hear the crashing of the waves at the tower's feet and around the rest of the city.

Before me stood a man sporting a shock of red hair almost identical to mine but cut short and a smile that lit up his face and eyes as he gazed at me. Red stubble adorned his chin. The look on his face said everything that I needed to know about him. This was my father.

"Scarlet, you have grown into far more than even I dared hope you would become, but I wish to ask your forgiveness. The start you had in life..." He shook his head as he looked down, ashamed. "No child should grow up thinking that they weren't wanted."

A part of me wanted to show anger at him, to make him regret leaving me like that, but I had seen the pain in my mother as well. It had eaten her alive, and my father had been dead my whole life anyway. Or near enough my whole life. I was better off letting it go. They did what they thought was best at the time, and we had all been forced to face the consequences of it.

"It's okay." I moved toward him. At my words, he raised his face again, and, wordlessly, we hugged.

It was strange to feel his embrace but at the same time know he wasn't there in the flesh. It was almost real enough that I felt warmth, emotion, and intention, but the physical sensation was off, as if he wasn't entirely there.

"I would have liked to have lived a life getting to know you," I added. "But neither of us got that luxury. To see you now is more than I'd have hoped."

"When the ancestors felt your presence coming and hoped you sought information and aid, no one doubted my right to respond. So here I am. I would wish to spend hours with you here, but the night is when the divide between our worlds is most... thin. There is not much time left. Tell me, why have you approached?"

"I seek counsel of a sort. And maybe, in some ways, approval."

"The approval you already have. We've given it and it will remain as long as you continue to do as you have begun and follow your heart. We already know that you have a good heart and care for those around you, even those who might not deserve it. What counsel do you need? I will do my best to provide it."

I explained to him everything that was happening with Grigick, what I suspected of his powers, his relations, and if he had everything needed to be the king. And then I asked the big question.

"Did he fail to connect to all of you or did you refuse his call? If he cannot connect to you at all..."

"He connected to us. He can use the magic, but none of the ancestors here wished to answer him in the way we answered you. It requires great effort to cross the divide, even at night. And we have already passed our power on to you. In time we could pass power on to another, and if something happened to you, we would empty ourselves to protect the world if needed, but it has not."

"So you essentially found him wanting?" I asked.

"Yes. As have you. Have you not told me that this dragon is a liar and willing to put others in danger without thought for what they risk just to be king? We would not bless a monarch such as this."

I nodded, grateful to hear something so clear coming from him. I hadn't been sure.

"Can you detect that in him as well?"

"Ah, you worry that you shouldn't judge." My father sat and took one of my hands in his. "Whoever he tried to connect to would have seen what was in his heart and his intentions, but even if they hadn't, we have been watching in the ways that we can. You have the support of the ancestors. Only you can do what is needed."

This was confirmation of a sort, but it wasn't very specific, and I looked away from my father, my eyes drawn to a carpet that wasn't part of my memory of the room.

"I'm sorry this burden has been placed on you. I'd understand if you didn't want it. There were many times that I wished I could be someone else and live a different life. But there is no one now. Only you can carry this burden. Our kind were foolish and turned on their saviors, removing our kind from existence one by one."

My father's shoulders slumped, and I felt the weight of his words. If I was the last remaining pure red dragon, there was no long-term hope for our race or the planet. The magic abilities of the red dragons would die out with me.

"What can be done?" I asked my father. "Surely there is a way to continue our line or that of another red dragon. I cannot be the last in the entire world."

He tilted his head sideways, but I didn't see any hope on his face.

"Then what does it matter what I do?" I asked. "If I am the last, when I die there will be nothing to stop the demon slowly breaking free and taking the rest of the world with him."

"I don't know if something could be done before then.

It is a question I asked myself several times. What was the point in continuing on? I didn't know that you would have any powers of note. Your mother is not entirely pure. She's close and can wield our magic as Grigick can, but she struggled to learn."

"So I am not even a pure red. Not really." I exhaled, knowing it to be true but not having considered it. It made me think twice about judging Grigick for it and assuming nothing could be done, but I had no desire to make a child with Grigick just to have one with enough power to keep the gate protected.

"There may be other ways," my father added as if he guessed my line of thought. "But it is something to be thought of another time. This is not why you came to us."

"No." I refocused on the story I had been telling him. When I finished, I sat on a nearby chair. "I don't know how to unite everyone. How to stop everyone from refusing to aid me."

"Then don't." His words made my mouth fall open. I had so many questions that I wasn't sure which one to utter first.

"People will never all agree with you, and they will never all accept you, but you don't need them to. You just need a majority, and for the rest to not think that you're so evil you must be stopped at all costs. Some people can hate you even, but if they don't dare go against those who support you, then it doesn't matter."

"But there are more than a few who hate me." I wondered if he had been listening to me or not.

"There were many who hated me. And my father. And his mother. They do not mean much, even when they have the power to hurt you. Or worse. The only consideration you have to focus on right now is: can you repair the gate, and can you keep those who matter alive? So, can you?"

I didn't reply, thinking about my father's words. So far I was keeping the people that mattered alive, but that didn't mean I could keep doing so.

"We need to go back to the gate and try again."

"Yes. It will not be long before he breaks out if something isn't done." It was all the confirmation I needed from my father on this score as well.

As soon as everyone was rested as well as possible, we had to try again. But how did I get Grigick and his companions to cooperate? The moment I told them I was going to be queen after all, they would turn against me and refuse to help.

"I cannot stay any longer." My father stood, his eyes full of warmth, but concern and a hint of sadness had crept into his face. "The night is almost over and you must return to your friends."

"I still have so much more to say." I went to him and gave him another hug.

Although it didn't feel entirely real, he squeezed back. "I do as well, but I have time to tell you one last thing. Don't fight battles you don't have to. Focus on the main goal—defeating the demon and keeping him locked up. Everything else may seem pressing, but it matters far less what anyone calls you or thinks of you if you can sleep at night knowing that you kept your eyes on the right task."

I nodded, hoping I would remember his words and wishing we had more time so I could get advice from him on how to deal with Brenta and Capricia. The elders followed Brenta and the guards followed Capricia. If I could get even one of the pair to take me more seriously, I could change things in my favor.

For now, they were both backing Grigick publicly. But I got the feeling that their patience with him was wearing thin. Would they choose me if he failed them? Or would they go back to pretending it didn't matter and they didn't need any heir?

I was going to get the answers to those questions one way: go back down the mountain to everyone else and suggest a new course of action.

I didn't rush, but I didn't dawdle either. We'd been here so long that little was left of the night and the sky to the east was lightening. The plants still lit my way and I was grateful, feeling as if the ancestors still watched over me and were guiding my path, though the advice they had given me had been more vague than I'd hoped.

As I descended, I felt for the connections around me and gasped. The tugging in the pit of my stomach was gone, replaced with a strange full-up feeling instead. Where I had felt tired and on the edge of my energy limits before I had begun my climb to the ancestors, now I felt invigorated, more full of magic than I had ever been.

And I was more aware of everyone around me.

It was as if, once again, simply connecting to the ancestors and the magic they possessed had given me a greater sense of what I was capable of and what was open to me as a red dragon. The heady feeling lingered as I continued down to the group. Not only could I feel the magical connections to each of them, but I could feel more clearly how much magic they had left and what they were trying to do with it.

Many of them were sleeping on the main plateau, and that left their energy stores replenishing and not being used, something I could also feel. The magic came from everything around us, slowly passing into us where it was stored for later. Was this how I had gained so much in a short space of time? The island had fed it to me the way it was feeding the magic to my companions?

I monitored it as I walked the last little way. Neritas and several of the others were still awake when I came into view. Grigick was also still awake and standing in a group with my mother, Alitas, Capricia, Brenta, and Griffin.

Getting the vibe that they were either having a disagreement or were pissed off about something, I rushed over to them.

"Everything okay?" I asked in a hushed voice. "I expected most of you to be asleep by now. We'll have to leave soon."

"I've got two conflicting stories of what happened up on that mountain," Alitas replied. "Neritas here is telling me that Grigick was denied anything, and Brenta, Capricia, and Grigick are telling me that the ancestors blessed him and he's now ready to be king."

I raised an eyebrow as my mouth fell open. This was a situation I hadn't expected to walk into. I'd expected Grigick to make excuses. To demand to come back another time. Or stay here a day so he could try again tonight. But I hadn't expected a full-out lie about it.

The three of them glared at me as if challenging me to

do something about it while Neritas, Griffin, and Alitas looked on.

"Could I have a moment alone with these three, please?" I asked, making it clear I meant Grigick and his handlers.

"What do you three think you're trying to do?" Folding my arms across my chest, I felt like a parent telling off naughty children. Were they really going to lie about this to keep Grigick on a throne he didn't deserve?

Everyone looked at each other in awkward silence. Grigick soon dropped his gaze to his feet as if he was ashamed. Although I noticed it, I didn't draw attention to it.

"We all know that nothing happened up there. The ancestors didn't bless Grigick and he's no more powerful than he was before he went up." I said the words quietly, so only they could hear.

"But everyone else here now thinks otherwise. They have no reason to doubt us," Capricia replied. "So they will follow us back to the gate and you and everyone else will give Grigick another chance to prove that he is capable of being our king."

I paused again, taken aback by this. "You want to go back to the gate and try again to power it?"

"Yes. We all know it needs doing. But you will help Grigick do this." Capricia glared at me as if she somehow had enough leverage to make me comply.

Although I considered telling her to take a hike and informing everyone of the truth, my father's words echoed in my head. *Don't fight battles you don't have to*. Right now I didn't have to fight this battle.

"Okay. We can go back to the gate." I shrugged, not sure

what their game was exactly, but I knew one thing: I wanted the gate kept shut and I was almost entirely sure I was going to have to be the dragon who did it.

It was Capricia's turn to look shocked as she took a step back. Grigick also gave me his attention as if he hadn't expected me to be so reasonable. But Brenta stared at me, her eyes even more narrow, but she stayed quiet.

"You should all get some sleep. I'll deal with Neritas." I smiled and motioned to the tents that the guards had set up for us while we'd been trying to communicate with the ancestors.

Grigick didn't need more encouragement, and he returned to his tent without looking back, but Brenta stepped closer to me.

"If you try and claim anything other than Grigick succeeded, I will personally tell everyone in this group every vile, disgusting rumor I can about you and what you are capable of. I will do everything I can to see that you're not welcome in Detaris or any other dragon city ever again." Her voice was low and I was sure it was meant to be menacing, but it wasn't.

I fought back a laugh as I nodded, unable to speak in case I betrayed how I truly felt. Antagonizing her didn't seem wise, but I couldn't do more than assent nonverbally and hope she left soon.

"We should sleep." Capricia gently took Brenta's arm. "So we have some energy to face tomorrow ourselves. It will be another long day."

As they walked away from me, Alitas, Griffin, and Neritas came back.

"What is going on?" Alitas looked as angry as I'm sure Brenta had wanted to look, and for a moment I hesitated.

"They're lying, but I've opted to let them lie. It's not worth fighting them when tomorrow will prove them full of shit all on its own." I hoped Neritas would understand and Alitas could accept the ruse long enough to let it play out.

"I think you've got some explaining to do if we're going to make this work." Alitas motioned for me to join him beside the nearby fire, and I noticed several packs of marshmallows and crackers stacked by a log. At least I could eat while I told them the new plan.

CHAPTER TWENTY-ONE

While the sun slowly made its appearance, I told my friends everything that had happened. Flick and Ben came to join us partway through, also confused by Grigick and what he had claimed. By the end of our conversation, they agreed that they would bide their time for now and allow this strange situation to play out.

Being able to feel the magic in everyone made it clear that most had recovered, although only I and the dragons who had accompanied me to the very top of the mountain were completely recharged. And it didn't include Grigick, Capricia, or Brenta. If anything confirmed that the ancestors hadn't blessed this red dragon, the lack of power they sported now was it.

Of course, my mother and I were the only dragons who could directly sense the magic in another, so no one else could tell that Grigick and his supporters were still weakened from the day before and the rest of us had been recharged simply by coming to the island.

I tried to get a little sleep before we would have to

leave, but Alitas soon ordered the honor guard to get us all some breakfast and start taking down the camp. Trying not to grump at him for doing so, I fetched some food and got Neritas back up again.

He frowned even more deeply than I had at being woken mere minutes after going to sleep, but I handed him another cereal bar and helped him to his feet.

"Remind me to take a day off as soon as we've secured your crown," he said quietly enough only Flick and I would hear.

"A day off? I don't think any of us know what that is. And I'm pretty sure my crown will never be entirely secure."

"When we've put this pretender in his place, then. We'll spend a day on the yacht. Tell everyone that you're on some pre-crowning ritual or rite of passage or something."

I grinned but didn't respond. He was still so convinced that I was going to be queen and everything would click into place. I had to focus on the gate and not on trying to be a hero or some great leader of the world.

The honor guards were more efficient at packing than I hoped they would be, and our entire camp full of dragons was soon making our way down the side of the mountain. I'd never been there in daylight before, but I was glad to be there now.

Everywhere I looked was covered in vibrant colors and the lush green of many different living plants. It was beautiful and made me pause at the head of our group.

"Can't remember the way back?" someone called from behind me. I ignored them, not even needing to consider it.

Just as some knowledge deep in my mind had guided my feet here, I instinctively knew the way back.

"We shouldn't linger too long," Neritas said. "Who knows what will be happening on the shore? The longer we are here, the more the enemy can build forces to attack us."

He had more of a point than I wanted to hear, but I listened to his advice and got moving. Each step led us deeper into the forest, but where the route upward had been full of twists, turns, and many different paths away from the center of the island, the way back appeared clearer.

No matter how difficult it had been to navigate up, leaving was simple. I was able to take whichever route led away from the center even if it twisted around before joining another path. With the lack of complication adding confidence to my feet and the downhill path making it easier for everyone who followed, we made good time back to the boats.

We again split into five groups, and I steered for Grigick and his supporters. We passed out more food. Everyone was hungry and our supplies were dwindling. When we had set out the previous day from Detaris, none of us had anticipated being away from a safe haven for so long. But one mission had led to another.

Now we were going back to attempting the first one. With any luck, we could plan a better approach a second time.

The journey back to the shore in the boats was tense. Even in the sunlight, the fog was thick around the base of the island and the rocks were treacherous. I couldn't see any better than I had been able to at night, but somehow I knew the way out anyway. And even if I hadn't, my mother knew the correct path.

In the light of day, everyone appeared to be more relaxed than they had on the way in, but it was also probably a byproduct of them thinking Grigick had been blessed. I'd said I'd stand aside if he was, and he'd claimed it to be true. Only a few of us knew that was a lie right now, and all of us were acting as if it weren't.

As we rowed back out of the rocky area and onto the open lake, I thought about Grigick and what he thought he could get away with. I wanted to get him alone and see if this was all Brenta and Capricia or if he was as enthused by this crazy plan as they were. More than once I'd caught him looking to them for guidance on how to respond to decisions he should have been confident of.

But we were a group of almost forty dragons, all going to the same place. Getting anyone alone wasn't going to be easy.

When we were close enough to shore that I could feel for the shadow catchers nearby, I closed my eyes for a moment and focused. If we were heading toward danger in the form of more demons sooner than later, I wanted to know about it so we could be prepared.

No matter how far I tried to reach with my mind, however, and for how long I concentrated, there was nothing. No sense of dread, not a single whisper of the monsters that clouded my thoughts more often than not. They hadn't even come close to the lake.

By the time we reached the shore, the sun was fully in the sky and it looked as if it was going to be another hot one. I frowned, knowing it would take its toll on all of us in yet another way. We had no protection from it while on the way to the gate, or at the gate, and many of the group were no longer young.

"We need to pick up supplies if we're going straight to the gate," Alitas said as soon as my feet were on dry land again.

I nodded, having anticipated it. For once, neither Brenta nor Capricia objected to us coming up with a plan to solve the problem. It was a relief when Alitas took control. With so little sleep since leaving Detaris, I was struggling to make simple decisions, even with all the magic flowing through me.

Alitas soon found somewhere on his phone where we could stop a little off the route back to the gate. No sooner had he suggested it than we were encouraged back to the cars, and I was sandwiched between Neritas and Flick once more.

"You look like shit, Red. Get some sleep while the rest of us worry about life and the future of the throne." Neritas grinned and lowered his shoulder, shifting so I could get comfy if I wanted to.

Normally I wouldn't have wanted to encourage any familiarity between us, but I felt as bad as I apparently looked, and knew I needed it if I was going to function and take on the shadow catchers yet again. I tilted my head his way, letting him cushion me while I got some sleep.

The car stopped and woke me up who knew how long later, and Neritas and Flick were quick to get out and stretch their legs. I stayed where I was a moment longer, trying to blink the sleep from my eyes and get a bearing on where I was. While I sat in the shadows of the car, I felt for danger with my mind.

I felt a few of the monsters that haunted my life, but they were far off and unmoving, at the very edges of my reach. With any luck, they wouldn't notice us and we would slip through the net and get to the gate before their commander knew we were near.

We'd stopped at a large wholesale store, and Alitas was ordering his guards to get what he thought we needed. I wasn't sure he could get everything he wanted—I didn't think such places stocked weapons suitable for fighting monsters—but I wasn't about to argue. If Grigick was our new king, I was an honor guard now and that made Alitas my boss as much as everyone else's. And If I was taking the throne, Alitas was responsible for keeping me and everyone with me safe, so I could let him handle it either way.

Many of the group went to a nearby coffee shop to get drinks and snacks and take a comfort break, but Grigick held back. Flick offered to get me a muffin and hurried away, almost sensing my intentions.

With so few people left around, it was easy for me to casually meander to the would-be king. He was standing near his car, trying to look as if he just wanted to stretch his legs. It allowed me to get fairly close to him before he noticed I was coming.

The second he spotted me he looked around for

Capricia and Brenta, but neither of them was nearby and he had no one else he was close to who would come to join us swiftly enough.

"Don't worry, I don't bite," I said when he still didn't look comfortable.

"But you are not happy with me either." Grigick kept his gaze on my face, his stance still on edge enough that he made it clear he would run if I caused trouble.

"I've come over here to try to understand you better, that's all. This whole situation is... baffling and I want to make sure that no one dies because of it."

"Always trying to make out that you care." The exasperation and anger in his tone took me by surprise.

"You have your window to take the throne." I shrugged, trying to keep calm despite how angry the whole situation made me in turn. He was playing with people's lives to win a crown that would mean nothing if he failed. "It's not my fault now if you fail. I've given you every opportunity I've had, and extra chances to prove yourself. As has everyone else with us."

"So what is it you don't think you understand?"

"Why do you think that you're going to succeed, when the ancestors didn't bless you and you failed miserably last time?"

As I spoke, Grigick folded his arms across his chest. "Are you threatening to tell everyone that the ancestors didn't respond to me and undermine all this? Because I did get a response."

"You can tell the others that lie if you want to and you can even try to tell Brenta and Capricia that they didn't ignore you, Grigick, but we both know the truth, really. If they'd responded to you, then you would be more powerful already and you wouldn't be running on a half-empty tank of magic."

Grigick's eyes narrowed at this, but he had the good sense not to respond and provoke me further. He didn't have a leg to stand on and he knew it. That's why he had been so nervous when I approached.

"I know Brenta and Capricia are putting pressure on you as well." I studied him as I added this bit, not as sure as I was acting but wanting to see if he'd confirm it. He gave nothing away. "If they're making you do this for the wrong reasons, then I hope that you can find some bravery to—"

"I'm not a coward." Grigick almost growled the last word and shook his head as he turned to walk away.

"Wasn't calling you one. But I know Brenta and Capricia well enough to know how forceful they can be."

"You don't know anything about either of them. Or me. You got lucky. Won the birth lottery and don't have to prove yourself to anyone. They all just fall in line for you and do as you say. Well, some of us have to earn what we've got and keep fighting for it. So if you think I'm going to tell everyone you can just have the keys to the kingdom, you can go take a hike."

Given that the last hike we'd been on had almost gotten us killed and the next one might as well, I wasn't sure it was a sensible choice of words, but I got the message. Even if I hadn't, Grigick deflated as he shook his head and strode toward the coffee shop.

I watched him go, not sure I'd handled the conversation well. If anything, it seemed to have made it worse and made him dig his heels in even more. Before I could move from beside his car, Ben joined me. He held a coffee and had brought me a tea.

"Tried to get the kid to see sense?" Ben asked.

"Tried to. Failed miserably."

"He's in too deep and got too much pride and pressure. Never a good combination. We'll just have to rescue him when he falls flat on his face again." Ben looked calmer than I'd seen him in ages, and I marveled at how he could be. We were about to face more shadow catchers than we could handle, for the second time in two days.

After a pause, I replied, "If he falls flat on his face, we won't know for sure that he can't do this. He's got all of us backing him up simply so we don't die in the process."

"And everyone else will see that it's you saving us and not him. Just like last time. These dragons aren't marching into danger to give him the opportunity to get them all killed. They're going to fight demons alongside you. Because they know that you're the best hope they've got and even if he screws this up the way they fear, you'll make sure we all get out alive."

I blinked, not sure how to respond to Ben's statement. Was that really what they were all thinking about me?

Did I have the loyalty and faith of all the dragons bar the few pushing to crown Grigick? I couldn't exactly ask them one by one or even as a group. It wasn't something I could ask any of them, no matter how much I wanted to know where I stood and if I had their support. I let it go and focused on the most important task. Keeping us all alive.

CHAPTER TWENTY-TWO

With the group resupplied and rested again, we were as ready as we were ever going to be for a day in the sun fighting our way across the demon-controlled ground to the gate, so we got back on the road.

We were only a half hour out from the parking lot, and before we were even halfway there I was trying to sense the shadow catchers. No doubt my mother would be doing the same a few cars behind us, and if Grigick had any sense, he'd have been doing it as well in the final car of our convoy.

The more of us who knew what we'd be up against in advance, the better.

I was surprised to find there weren't many more of the creatures lingering nearby, as I had feared. I guessed there were no more than we'd left alive the day before. To be sure, I kept concentrating, closing my eyes again and pushing my abilities as hard as I could for a couple of seconds.

The way was clearer than I'd expected. Opening my eyes, I mentioned this to the dragons with me.

"It's a good sign, given we don't have all the dragons with us we had last time. Sarai is too exhausted and hurt and many of the most injured are staying with her at the farmhouse," Alitas replied. "But more demons could be near the gate so let's not assume this is going to be easier just yet."

He had a point. We'd been ambushed coming back from the gate on a previous occasion. When we'd thought we were relatively safe. I had to make sure we didn't get mobbed again. On the way back we would be far weaker, all our magic channeled into the gate itself. At some point, I would have to judge when we had given it enough and we needed to return. No one else in the group would have enough information to make the call.

I thought about this, hoping the number of shadow catchers remained low as we drove closer and closer to their hub. More than once I considered telling Alitas not to stop. To drive past the entrance to the parking lot and head for Detaris or one of the other dragon cities instead. Who was I to ask everyone to risk their lives? More to the point, could I let them make that choice with a clear conscience, knowing it was based on an outright lie? Right now, most of them believed Grigick was the chosen one and would be able to make the gate safe. What would happen when he tried and nothing changed for the better?

But no matter how much I worried that I was doing the wrong thing, my mouth wouldn't open and utter a sound. It was as if I wasn't in control.

Resigned to accept whatever followed, I focused on

keeping calm when the unease of the gate and all the demons that protected it came closer in my mind. I'd come a long way from running scared and hiding behind a dumpster from the first one I'd encountered. Now I was hunting them and taking an arsenal of skilled dragons and weapons with me.

By the time we stopped, I heard another helicopter in the air. Instead of following us as they had the previous day, intent on putting me in the news, they were hovering over the gate. Now it was so large and rotten that it was being picked up by the human world.

A part of me wanted to pull out my phone, check the news and get an idea of what everyone was saying, but it was a distraction I couldn't afford. I hoped the human world didn't believe magic was real and that they thought this was just a strange curiosity. Despite that, I couldn't ignore them forever. I promised myself I'd focus on how to get them to forget we existed as soon as I knew the gate wouldn't open and the planet was safe.

"Can you charge everything up?" Alitas asked as another pair of honor guards came into the parking lot from a side path. Both of them carried multiple shields on their backs and had armfuls of swords, spears, and daggers. The one on the left even had three bows slung over one shoulder and several quivers of arrows hanging from his belt.

I raised an eyebrow, wondering where this stash had come from. I had been to the only weapons cache in the area I'd thought existed. Despite my curiosity, I did as Alitas asked and reached for the magic in the dragons all around me. Whether they liked me or not, I connected to their magic and tugged on a little from everyone, taking more from those who had it to give and less from the others.

After so many fights and situations where I needed to draw on the strength of those around me, it was almost second nature to me now. My mind compensated for the relative strengths so I didn't drain any one dragon entirely.

With several hours on the road and plenty of food along the way, most of the dragons were close enough to their full capacity that I needn't have worried, but Brenta and Grigick were still lower than expected after all the recovery time they'd had. No doubt the red dragon had been using some of his own as he tried to work out how to do half the tricks I knew.

With all this running through my head, I added magic to everything before me, connecting to all the items and taking a bow and several arrows from the new guard. Knowing Flick as well as I did, I handed it to him. His face lit up as he took it and slung a quiver of arrows at his waist as well.

"All of you get in your places," Alitas commanded, the only one of us who could issue an order and know everyone would listen to it whether they agreed or not. He was the captain of the honor guard and had pledged to serve whoever ended up in charge and keep us all alive until we'd settled that score between us. Neutral enough but also powerful.

I moved to the front of the line, catching Brenta's gaze for long enough to see the anger in her eyes. No matter what I did, she never liked me. For now, I pushed that thought aside. We had a gate to fix and strengthen and it was going to start with another hike through the forest while our minds wrestled with the weight of our own failures and unease and fear.

It weighed the body down physically as well as mentally, but it got easier to resist with time. You could only be confronted with your fears and everything wrong in your life so many times and not become hardened to it all on some level.

This time, it felt as if the weight of the world heaped on my shoulders as soon as I took a couple of steps. I exhaled, my legs aching as if I was trying to wade through molasses by the time I'd counted ten paces, and my entire body screaming after another ten.

"Are you okay, Red?" Neritas leaned in closer and kept his body slightly behind so he could support me.

"It's like he's hitting me with everything he's got this time," I replied through gritted teeth. "Something stronger than ever before."

"Then he must be directing it all at you. I feel nothing beyond the breeze in the trees."

I wasn't sure if this was good news or not. With some of our group wanting me to fail, I didn't feel as if I could show my weakness. I might not be able to help it if every bit of malice was aimed at me. Could I face that the entire way?

I didn't reply, trying to think and barely able to, counting steps and forcing my body to carry on moving even when most of me wanted to give up. As I carried on, Neritas slipped an arm around me. I felt Flick and Ben close behind and coming together to offer support.

Although I knew this was just a trick and it would fade when I got close enough to step into the main area of influence, it didn't make it easier to keep walking. Neritas wasn't going to let me stop. His grip on my waist grew firmer as I grew weaker.

Almost as suddenly as it began, the pressure slipped away, my body straightened, and my reliance on my friends lessened over the next ten paces until I couldn't feel the pressure at all. I looked at my closest companions, trying to work out what had happened. We still had a long way to go down the gate path and I was sure it couldn't be over yet. Had the demon exhausted his ability to hinder us already?

Before I could utter my question out loud, Jace groaned and stumbled. The guard beside her caught her, stopping her from going down, but it brought our group to a halt.

"It looks like he's going to test us one by one, but I'm not going to let him beat any of us," I called. "When it hits you, let us know and the dragons around you will support you and get you through. Trust those around you and look out for anyone struggling alone."

With that, Alitas moved down the group, slipping an arm around Jace as Neritas had just done for me.

"You've got this, just like you always have," he urged her.

She grimaced and took another step as we all carried on. Over the next ten minutes, the same thing happened to five more members of our group. Each one was suddenly overwhelmed and slowed to a crawl until the dragons around them rallied and helped. I did my best to keep us moving at an even pace, noticing that those who recovered never quite had the same energy to them as before being attacked.

This was brutal and I feared that we would lose several of our team along the way. When Griffin was hit next, he cried out and slumped to the ground.

"Keep everyone going forward," I told Neritas. I couldn't let anything happen to the first elder in Detaris who had stood up for me.

I hurried down the line, encouraging everyone to keep moving until I reached the older dragon. Gently, I put an arm around him, joining Alitas to help him to his feet. At the same time, I took some of the magic from the strongest of us and sent it toward Griffin, hoping it would boost him in a way that our physical presence couldn't.

"You've got this, Griffin. Just keep going a little further and the demon will give up."

He looked at me as if he wasn't convinced, but something gave him just enough fight to get his feet under him again and carry on. I didn't leave his side until the pained expression left his face and his breathing eased.

As he relaxed, the pressure gone from his mind, I looked to see who was hit next. Without hesitation, Alitas and I strode to the next dragon and the next. Even when Grigick, Capricia, and Brenta needed help, we went to them and spoke words of encouragement and lent them the strength of the group.

Step by painstaking step, we made our way closer to the gate and the threat until I paused about halfway and called for a break. With so many dragons needing my help and my focus on channeling magic to them, I hadn't been paying attention to the shadow catchers in the area.

I hoped my mother was monitoring them, even if Grigick couldn't, but I could feel their threat from farther away than either of them could, and the more warning we had of an attack the better. More of the creatures were nearby than there had been, but given how much closer we were to the gate, I wasn't surprised.

I took the opportunity to have a break as well at that point, pulling a snack from my bag and munching while I surveyed everyone. We'd gone about halfway, and more than half the group had been tested. I hoped that meant we'd get some relief once the demon had challenged all of us. But I also knew it was possible that some of us would have to face it twice.

Could we handle being hit twice? I knew I was terrified of what it would do. None of us were at our best.

Despite my fears, we couldn't linger too long either. The demon knew we were coming now, and that meant we had to carry on before he had too much of a chance to prepare. And all the while I heard the helicopter nearby again. They hadn't flown directly overhead and we'd been under the tree canopy when they did, but it was yet another threat.

I couldn't afford the distractions and didn't want them.

After giving everyone ten minutes, Alitas got up to encourage the group onward. It made him look like he was in charge again, not me. And Grigick and everyone else followed his lead without complaint. No sooner had we tried to get moving again than someone was hit with the mental weight of the demon's attack.

Once more, Alitas and I worked together to help the victims each time and keep them going. The few of us who had made the journey many times were still more resilient, but none of us could walk normally as if it was no difficulty, or pretend to find it easy.

Slowly the demon worked through our entire group, and the fear of what it might feel like to be hit with an attack mounted in the remaining dragons. Ben, Neritas, and Flick were some of the few left, along with Alitas himself. Harriet had also been left out of the attack for now and her eyes darted from one target to the next.

She stumbled a couple of times, paying more attention to whoever Alitas and I were helping than the path ahead of her, and she was shaking when Ben got hit next and I passed her to get to him.

Ben grunted in pain as he tried to keep walking several paces unaided, appearing drunk and leaning to one side. Flick braced him, trying to get him through it until we were also there.

Although we needed most of our magic for the next stages of our mission, I used a little to help Ben. If all I did was take a little of the pain away from the dragons being hit hardest, it was worth it.

Neritas and Flick were next, one after the other. Neither of them held up quite as well as Ben, but they kept their feet moving and didn't lean on me and Alitas as much as others had.

Harriet and Alitas were the only ones not to be hit as Flick was finally released. I started to move to Harriet, knowing that Alitas wasn't far away and I could get to his side swiftly enough already.

It was the right call. My arm went around the young woman as she buckled. I caught her, and Alitas reached out for her a moment later. At first, she didn't move, her face screwed up in pain, but I softly called her name as Alitas handed his spear to the nearest honor guard so he could carry her if necessary.

"You've got this. I know it hurts, but you won't have to fight through it for long," I whispered to her, my mouth near her ear.

If she heard me, she made no sign or response, merely clung to Alitas. He was about to lift her and carry her along the path when she got her feet under her and took one step and then another.

The farther she went, the more the pressure appeared to ease until she was walking easily again.

We'd done it.

All of us had pushed through the pain and the mental attack to get toward the gate.

No sooner had I thought this than my own mind clouded again. I stumbled, almost crashing into Harriet, still beside me. I had just enough presence to see Alitas stumbling as well. Now two of us were being hit at once, and this much closer to the gate it was even worse than the first time.

I gritted my teeth, fighting back the whimpers of pain and despair I wanted to let out, closing my eyes and pushing my body forward anyway.

As I forced myself to keep moving, I was only vaguely aware of the people around me and the arms and hands that reached out to support me.

I'm not letting you beat me now, I thought as I fought through step by step.

I had no way to know if the demon could hear me, but that didn't stop me from promising to get to him anyway and getting my feet to fall back into rhythm. The attack seemed to go on a lot longer this time, and my mind went numb as I slipped into a pattern and focused on the monotonous movement needed to put one foot in front of the other.

After what seemed like another age, the pressure slowly eased and I could lift my head a little more.

"We're at the edge," Neritas called back. My stalwart friend had led us on even though I was no longer beside him. As he spoke, the pressure in my head eased, going away slower than it appeared, but giving me the relief I needed to get to the edge of the rotting area.

CHAPTER TWENTY-THREE

Once again, Alitas took charge, having recovered from his attack at about the same time I did. He motioned for everyone to stay in the column we'd already formed. It had worked well enough for us so far in terms of healing the land and getting everyone traveling across it, but it wasn't the strongest when it came to fighting shadow catchers.

"What are we up against, Red?" Alitas asked me in a low voice when everyone was ready and waiting to carry on again.

I was already trying to sense the shadow catchers. A few were waiting on the decayed circle ahead of us, but nowhere near as many as the last time we were here.

"I can't feel as many as I expected by now. A few more than we left after the fight yesterday. They're already moving toward us, however. Not all of them. But enough. We can't linger here. We'll need to either push through to hit some head-on before the others get here or go around the edge and head in from somewhere else."

Alitas considered my suggestion to go around the edge,

but he shook his head. "There's not another good path for miles. If we went that way it would take even more out of the group, the demon would be able to keep pressuring us, and we'd still have to go the whole distance to the center. Straight on gets us there as quickly as we can."

I wasn't going to argue with him when he knew the area better than anyone else. No one could tell me I wasn't being flexible or considering other options, and no one could blame me for not letting Grigick decide what to do. The final say wasn't down to me.

The entire walk from the cars to the edge of the demon's influence on the world, Grigick had been almost entirely silent and still wasn't acting in charge. I could have smacked him for how little he was doing to help or show that he was worthy of the throne. What good was a king who did nothing to help?

"All right, take us to the gate, Neritas." Alitas shifted to the side and out of the way so I could walk beside the green dragon.

Despite being only a few years older than me, Neritas was a powerful dragon with a great deal of control, and it didn't appear to trouble him to grow nature under our feet and ensure that the rot didn't get to us.

Now even more proficient in the task, Neritas soon had a plain, grass-like plant growing up ahead of us, and we stepped out and got on our way to the gate. This time, the monsters didn't attack us right away, but it was clear we were being watched, possibly to see if they could find a more vulnerable point to attack.

I could think of several points that I dreaded. When we had been on the small gate island long enough to be drained but still had to make a path back to the safety of the forest, we would make the easiest targets. A few weaker moments were coming up. Right now, when we had only just stepped out and had almost all our energy reserves to draw on, we were a formidable fighting team.

As if understanding this and making sure not to waste his resources, the demon kept his shadow catchers at bay. They weren't avoiding us—my mind caught several fluttering about the place—but they weren't coming at us directly either.

We moved as a group, keeping together and not pushing the abilities of our dragons to heal the land and stop it from hurting us as we crossed it. We needed them to be able to get us back as well, and it was easier for them to go slower.

Although I could see a couple of shadow catchers ahead, they drifted back slowly, keeping away from us and giving some ground as they did. It was the first time I had seen them so controlled. Normally they were either holding ground or attacking us. Retreating was something I'd only ever seen lone and injured demons do. And even then, only sometimes.

"You get the feeling that we're walking into another trap?" Neritas asked as he continued to transform the ground before me right before I stepped on it.

"The whole journey so far." I didn't take my eyes off the creatures ahead or lose concentration on my monitoring of the others.

As we got closer to the gate, the unease grew, the main demon's presence so close behind it that it leaked out into the environment around us. We had to keep going, however. If we didn't make it to the gate this time and fix some of the broken pillars, we were unlikely to get another chance.

To make matters worse, the helicopter that had been lingering in the distance was making its way closer, no doubt coming to film us and splash our entire trek all over the news. Making humanity believe it was fake was going to get harder and harder, and I hoped they would run out of fuel before they managed to film anything more than us walking.

Our magic was already on display, however. All our green dragons were healing the ground. Plants were springing up and growing, and moss formed a path for us to follow.

When we could see the gate and had more distance behind us than ahead of us, the shadow catchers finally made their move. They descended on us in force, all of them moving toward our group, rushing as fast as I'd ever seen them move.

"Incoming," I yelled, connecting mentally to every dragon's magic source and every weapon and shield we carried between us.

Neritas and I flung out the powered disks and caught the first two demons to approach us, stopping them in their tracks as they fried. It wasn't enough to kill them before we got there, but a slash from both our swords took their heads off and opened up the path to the gate again.

We grabbed the disks from the air in unison and I passed mine back toward Flick, letting him pick targets while I focused on channeling magic where it was needed. Although I tried to keep everyone moving forward at the same pace, as soon as shadow catchers got close to the sides of our group and came rushing up behind us, we slowed.

"Keep us moving," I told Neritas and urged Flick to take my place beside him. "I'll protect everyone and make sure we all follow on."

It wasn't my job alone to put myself in danger. Alitas and Kryos stepped out of rank as well. I strode toward the nearest monster, gripping my sword and feeling the power in it charge the surface once more. I hit the side of the monster as Alitas reached it from the other side. Skewering it between us and pinning it in front of Griffin allowed the elder to stab it with the spear he'd been given.

Although his weapon was far more rudimentary and couldn't hold its charge the way our swords could, he finished the demon off and it puffed into smoke and drifted off. I looked for the next monster and saw a gap in our chain had appeared ahead of Griffin when he'd paused to fight. I darted through the gap to block a beak as another shadow catcher attacked Brenta.

She stumbled backward, almost bumping into Capricia and getting in the way of Grigick. The whole chain stopped and I growled as I used my shield to shove the shadow catcher back and away from one of the more vulnerable dragons in our group.

This time, Grigick tried to help in battle, no longer hiding among his honor guards, but he was crude in his attacks, slashing at the demons when they were still out of reach or veering away to attack another and barely using his shield in time. It forced his honor guards to stick close to him and protect him either way. I wasn't sure what approach was better—him letting them get on with it or trying to help and failing.

I couldn't afford to spare it a thought as I fought onward and tried to defend everyone who needed it. More of the monsters were coming our way, and if we didn't get to the gate soon, we were going to be overwhelmed and forced to flee once more.

I hurried everyone on, routing some of our magical energy to the green dragons with us and hoping everyone could match the faster progress. Neritas was doing everything he could to open a forward path, and several of the other dragons had widened it to give everyone room to fight and dodge attacks.

Having learned from some of the struggles the previous day, Alitas and his honor guards rotated around the group, keeping the weaker ones moving and making sure none of the demons got as close.

Slotting myself into the guard pattern, I sent my strikes where they could be used best, and we got everyone moving again. My mother added her expertise as more of the demons came in close. She was no longer defending the rear of the group, having left that to Reijo and Merrik.

Although I had been filled with energy and hope from the ancestors in the night, my body soon began to ache. I hadn't slept enough to be fighting physically, and the drain on my body to get to the area around the gate had taken a toll.

I will admit that you are persistent, but you have little loyalty from your companions. For a leader, you are more of a sacrificial lamb. Do you think they care if you survive this?

Shaking my head, I tried to ignore the voice of the

demon. He wanted to taunt me, make me believe all sorts of things, and play on my insecurities. I couldn't believe him. But I gulped nonetheless and questions formed in my head before I could push them all away.

Alitas hadn't moved to help another dragon fight the demon's influence until after I had recovered. At least the first time. Plenty of hands had reached out to support me the second time, I reminded myself.

Either way, I couldn't let anyone die on my watch. I had vowed to protect everyone who came here with me and I'd known then that some of them hated me, not even putting on any pretense. I had to stick to what I promised myself. Not because it would gain me any favor with them, but because I needed to live with my own conscience.

As I ended another monster and sent it swirling into smoke, I took a moment to look around and feel for the danger. The gate wasn't far off now, and if we could time it right we might get a clear run toward it. Several shadow catchers still lurked nearby, however, and a few more would get to us before we could find a gap in the fighting to urge everyone to run.

"Make the whole path and hold it," I yelled loud enough that every green dragon would hear me. I didn't care if Grigick or Alitas were meant to be in charge at this point. We needed to get to safety.

I stepped out of formation, using my magic to propel my tired limbs faster and get me where the fighting was at its worst: back by Grigick. He had a monster on either side of the group, neither of them being dealt with fast enough.

Bringing my sword down on the neck of one, I cut its head off and ignored the smoke to sprint behind him and attack the other. The second appeared to anticipate my approach and lunged my way. I got my shield up just in time to save myself from being stuck through the middle but it hit the metal shield with a loud clang and the force made my arm go numb for a moment.

I carried on, not daring to take my eyes off the enemy or adjust my grip, but shoving it back and hacking at it as quickly as I could.

With the honor guard beside me recovering, he stabbed at it as well, lodging his spear in the side of the monster and holding it still for just long enough that I could hit it. Alitas came up next, adding the killing blow and saving me from having to block another attack.

Together we moved along the edge of the group, flinging ourselves at the only remaining shadow catcher on this side. It didn't stand a chance between us and Kryos, who was already keeping it from attacking Brenta.

"Run," I shouted when we finished sending it back where it had come from.

They all obeyed. Even Capricia did as I asked and ran the last fifty yards to the gate. Neritas and the green dragons, now spread out, hadn't quite finished making a path to the gate, but they managed to stay ahead of everyone and join our safe haven up with the stone of the gate area soon enough that everyone could sprint for it.

As soon as they were safely on the stone, the honor guard formed a circle around the rest of the dragons, their ranks growing as everyone arrived and the green dragons could stop using their magic and focus on aiding us in battle as well.

I held out until almost everyone was beyond me, using

the green dragons' magic to help hold the path and relieve more of them sooner. My mother and Alitas were the last alongside me, all three of us running to safety beside each other. Finally, we stepped onto the stonework and everyone relaxed, panting and holding a circle of spears, swords, and shields.

Almost as if they sensed our extra strength, the shadow catchers stopped as well, wary suddenly and no longer reckless.

"Keep an eye on them, but let's get closer to the gate and get our job done," I said to Alitas and the other honor guards.

Before I had even finished speaking, Grigick pushed his way forward and motioned for me to get out of his way. "I wish to see what I must fix."

His eyes narrowed as he studied me and I didn't move. Now that we weren't being attacked and I had put everything into getting us here, he wanted to be in charge again.

As a few more shadow catchers came our way, I stepped aside.

"Fix what you can then while I help keep us all safe." I joined the honor guard and city guards as Alitas and Capricia had them spread out at regular intervals around the stone haven.

I tried not to worry about how little Grigick could help us and instead focused on the bigger picture. Every shadow catcher I sent back to the abyss was one less to hurt us, and I could do it more efficiently than most. It would save us energy, which we could use to power the gate.

CHAPTER TWENTY-FOUR

Panting, I killed my third shadow catcher in as many minutes. Several of them rushed me as if they were trying to overwhelm me and break through to the more vulnerable dragons behind me.

My sword and shield were still about half charged, and I had lost count of how many demons I had killed in the last two days. My limbs were tired, but if this worked, it would be worth it.

During a lull, the light breeze wafted away the smoke from my kills. For some time now I had been able to sense a different presence to the demons attacking us. I feared Fintar was back, but I reminded myself that he had fallen in battle several months ago. Whoever lurked out on the rot, though, I was pretty sure they were another handler.

I pulled out of the defensive circle, calling Kryos to swap places with me so I could go see what was coming in that direction. It appeared to be a handler, someone with a humanoid body walking slowly closer with shadow catchers around them forming an honor guard.

They paused a few hundred yards away, the shadow catchers forming a circle at a similar distance out from us as more and more came into the area.

"Keep an eye on them and let me know the second they move," I said to the nearest honor guard before I fell out of position and approached the circle holding the gate itself.

Grigick was standing by one of the pillars, his eyes closed and his face screwed up in intense concentration.

Near him, Brenta and Griffin were both fussing and trying to work out if they could detect a difference in the power the pillars had.

I rolled my eyes and moved to Jace and Cios, who were working with their group to fix one of the broken pillars. They had been researching how to fix them and had brought several strips of metal that could be welded in place to form the new conduit line for the magic they needed to store.

How the pillars, weapons, and armor stored magic was still a mystery. If books had been written about it, they had been long lost to time or were in the well-guarded secret part of the library in Detaris. Ben and I hadn't had access to that since the translation book we'd borrowed had gotten soaked in a river while running away from shadow catchers.

When I drew closer, Jace glanced up at me. "You coming to help or watch?"

"Help, if there's anything I can do." I didn't hesitate. We needed this to work.

"Can you connect to it and let us know if it's channeling the energy from the rest of the pillar?"

I nodded and stepped closer. It was easy to connect to

the two parts, the section they were trying to weld and the pillar already there, but the pillar was so damaged I couldn't feed it, and the new part wasn't connected enough yet that they were sharing energy.

Not daring to charge the new metal, I told Jace what I felt and let her work with Cios and her team to fix it.

Before they could make much more progress, Grigick came over.

"The pillars are more charged than before," he announced as if it was something to be proud of.

I connected to them as well, but I could barely feel the difference, and the dragons with us were still holding a lot of their magic. Only the fight had drained any of us so far.

Taking a step back, I wondered what to do. If I charged the pillars now and used all our magic, everyone would believe Grigick had done it. But if I didn't add to their reserves, we would have come all this way and risked our lives for almost nothing.

As I considered the two possibilities, Grigick caught my gaze. I could see the amusement in his eyes. He knew the position he'd just put me in. He knew I had to make him look competent or run the risk of the gate failing. And the entire planet depended on the gate not failing. I couldn't do anything but help.

I closed my eyes for a moment, making sure I had all the connections I needed to everyone's magic and the working pillars able to be filled. At first, I went slowly, wary of drawing too much, but when several heads turned my way I realized they could tell it was me and not Grigick.

I shrugged. At least some of them would have heard

Grigick declare himself finished powering a pillar. If they hadn't felt the same tug of magical energy from him, they wouldn't need me to explain that he'd lied and had faked being able to fix this.

Seeing his plan had backfired, I relaxed into doing what I needed and drew about a third of the power the dragons had, feeding it into the pillars.

I didn't dare take more than that. We would have to fight our way back to safety again and there would be more pillars to strengthen if they could be physically fixed.

With that done, I moved back toward Jace and checked her work. It felt different, with a small connection there.

"I think you are getting there," I said. "But it still needs to be connected better."

"The metal needs to be incredibly hot to weld it together. I've only managed a small section," the dragon beside Jace said, not looking up from her work. It was taking a long time, and Grigick moved closer.

"Let me begin charging it while you work. We shouldn't linger here."

"No!" I tried to stop him in case the magic flowing between the two parts when they weren't fully connected broke it, but he didn't listen.

Within seconds I heard it humming, and the noise grew more intense.

"Stop." I moved toward him to yank him away from it, not sure what else to do. Even if I pulled him back, I had no way to sever his connection entirely. It was mental and he hadn't even placed his hands on it.

Before I could even get my hands on him, the pillar shattered and the metal splintered, breaking the old piece even more and sending the new one flying up and out of Jace's hands.

Everyone gasped or yelped in pain as we were hit with chunks of brick or shards of rusted metal. I brought my shield up to deflect some, but I was mostly too late.

Immediately my mother rushed over, pulling the healing device she carried from her bag. Dropping my shield a moment, I reached for mine as well. As I did, I noticed a sliver of metal sticking out of my leg. It stung, but I didn't think it had done too much damage, and I was far more concerned about Jace, who was holding out two bloodied palms, both sliced up by the fresh metal she had been trying to weld in place.

I hurried to her as my mother went to the woman who had been welding. Her torso was covered in tiny shards. Thankfully, most seemed to be stuck in her apron and not her body, but my mother didn't waste a single moment beginning to heal her.

With the magic of all the dragons already flowing through me, I had more than enough to fuel the healing device. I quickly ran it over Jace's hands, doing a quick pass over both to begin the healing and take a lot of the pain away before I did anything else.

As I worked, Jace's face relaxed, and her breathing became more even.

"Thanks, Red. You're a useful dragon to have around."

I didn't respond but several of us shot Grigick glares. He was standing in a huddled group with Brenta, Capricia, and a couple of city guards who had stepped out of place. They had another healing device, but unless Grigick could get it working, it would do him no good. And I wasn't going to help.

As soon as Jace's body had done all it could and the healing device had sped up her natural ability to protect herself, I moved to Cios and helped him as well. He had several shards sticking out of his arm. Somehow he had anticipated it just enough to turn and take the blow to the side of his body and not the front.

"This might hurt." I needed to pull the shards out to heal the wounds.

"It's okay. Do what you need to." Cios gave me a brief nod as I took the first one in my hands and pulled it from his body. Blood began to pour from the wound, but I had the healing device ready and I got it to stem the bleeding quickly enough. He soon exhaled in relief.

"I'll echo Jace. You're a useful dragon in a pinch," he said. "And I'm very glad we're doing this with you here."

"You're going to have to hurry up the healing," Alitas yelled. "The handler has decided they've waited long enough."

I growled, not entirely surprised. They were always going to pick the moment when we were weakest. For all the good I had done in powering up the depleted pillars, one of them was more damaged than before and it was probably weaker than ever. All because Grigick had decided to show off while I was doing his job for him.

Yet again, he had shown himself to be an incompetent leader and made my job harder.

With Cios mostly healed and my mother free from helping the others, she took over.

"Go kill some demons and put that handler in his

place," she ordered me as she picked up my shield and handed it back to me. I hadn't healed myself, but I rushed to the edge of the gate nearest the handler anyway, shoving my healing device in my pocket.

Neritas was already there, his disks in his hands. I pulled mine out again and the two of us aimed at the handler, waiting until he was close enough that we had a chance of hitting him.

Although I threw first, Neritas was a fraction of a second behind me. A shadow catcher came across the handler before mine could find their target, but they fried the demon and it puffed into smoke just before Neritas' got there. The handler dodged them and they hit another demon behind.

"That's two less to kill," Flick said as he lifted his sword.

"Form up to defend, everyone." I stepped right to the edge. Most of the demons were coming at me, and I braced myself for the first impact.

"We might as well go," Jace called from the pillars. "The shattering metal broke the blow torch. We can't fix anything else."

I swore as I realized what that meant. We hadn't made it any better coming here. We'd made it worse. We could do nothing but fight our way out and hope the gate held long enough to come back.

Again.

No matter what we tried, it seemed doomed to failure, and almost entirely because Brenta and Capricia insisted on doing everything their way.

"I hope you're all happy with what your actions have

led to," Reijo said to the small group. Grigick was still focused on healing himself.

Although I wanted to say something similar, I wasn't sure that now was the right time to berate them. Whatever had happened, we needed to get to safety, and that meant all of us working together.

"Everyone form up into travel formation. Get your weapons ready and don't leave anyone behind. I'm getting us out of here and I don't want to hear a single word of argument about it," Alitas shouted.

It took a little while before the group got back into the same line of pairs, and the shadow catchers descended on us before then. The honor guards, Neritas, Flick, and I fought hard, creating a wall of shields briefly and stabbing over the top of it.

With so many coming at us at once, their powerful tails caught a couple of us off guard, including me. I hissed in pain, clenching my jaw shut to keep from being more vocal.

Neritas rescued me, stabbing the monster before it could strike again.

"Get your mom to heal you up, too, or you're no good to us fighting our way out of here. You're too hurt now."

Although I didn't want to look down and check, I was in enough pain that I was pretty sure he was right. As Flick moved his shield over and sidestepped partially into the space I had occupied, I knew I didn't have much choice.

I moved backward, but I paused a moment and checked they could hold the line without me. I had my healing device in my pocket, and my mother quickly fell out of line as well, intending to help me and make it twice as fast.

While I healed the wound from the demon, my mom pulled out the sliver of metal and focused on that wound. It stung as she yanked, but she soon had it healed.

Within a minute, we had done what was needed to get me back into the fray. I tucked the healing device away once more, hoping it wouldn't be needed again today but aware it probably would, and put myself back on the front lines.

CHAPTER TWENTY-FIVE

Back in the familiar grouping, I soon led the dragons off the safe haven in the middle of the rotten land. I tried not to think about how much worse the situation was now.

Neritas didn't need me to give him the go-ahead to start healing the land back toward the safety on the other side. We needed to get out of here, but we were going to be vulnerable while we fled.

The handler was the biggest threat to us. He appeared human-like at first, but as we got closer I saw that he was more like Fintar. Not entirely human, and holding his form less well as the battle intensified.

The honor guards moved toward the front of our group, spreading out a little and getting our green dragons to make us a wider path through the rotting land. I channeled energy to all of their weapons and shields and sent lightning crackling out from my sword before I engaged with each monster.

It was fun to use so much raw power and push back one of the monsters before it could attempt to strike us, but it was an abuse of energy that I wouldn't be able to keep up. The tricky part was figuring out whether this strategy was worth it. Fighting for ages and doing it on our own strength might be possible, especially if I could take out the handler before he hurt anyone else. We had already killed so many of them.

The cost of fighting without much aid could be too great, however. If anyone died and I could have saved them, or we had loads of magical strength left and could have killed more shadow catchers, I would feel awful and wish I had done more.

Somehow, I had to find the balance. And I had to do it while fighting as many of these monsters as I could.

I slashed down on the neck of one aiming for Neritas, severing the head and puffing it into smoke before it could do more than strike his shield with its beak.

Within seconds another took its place, and I had even less time to bring my shield up and block the attack from a monster near me.

Despite the relentless attacks, we pushed forward, slowly making headway toward the tree line that represented safety. The handler kept back, encouraging his minions toward us in a thick enough wave that we couldn't get through them to take him on.

I stabbed and slashed and pierced the shadow monsters wherever I could do damage, all while funneling magic and powering the shields and weapons of almost every dragon in our group. Even with us fighting so fiercely, the group started to bunch up, the weakest encircled by the strong, and none of us were able to move forward fast enough to get out of there.

Even with all of the shadow catchers coming at us, we were pushing forward and their numbers were dwindling. I needed to think of something to punch through, and I needed to do it swiftly.

"We need to take out that handler," Alitas said as he fought his way over to me. "I don't know how much steam you have left, but we're not going to manage it without you."

"Can you get me closer?" I asked. "Cut me a path somehow?"

"If we maybe split the group," Neritas replied before the captain of the honor guard could respond.

"I'll keep this group safe," Kryos offered. "And get that useless excuse of a red dragon to help us out while Scarlet does what she needs to."

It seemed a plan had formed with the right combination of allies, and my chance to take on the handler and punch through materialized on its own. A few more dragons volunteered to come with me so I had at least one of every color and all the abilities I could need to fuel our attacks. We also gained a couple more green dragons— Alitas had brought significantly more green honor guards than any other type, and Cios didn't want to be far behind the main action.

We were going to need them as we cut a narrow path and moved away from the group. With Neritas and me at the front and the ground quickly growing lush and green ahead of us, we used our charged-up shields to repeatedly shove the shadow catchers out of the way and to the sides. Alitas and Jace were on one side, and Ben and Flick on the other, all four stabbing the monsters before they could recover.

Cios and the honor guards with him protected our rear and finished off the monsters that got past us.

With all of us focused on making progress, the shadow catchers could do little to stop us. But the handler continued to back away.

Knowing we were a threat that could get to him easily if we broke through the press of drone-like monsters, the handler changed his strategy as well. Almost all of the shadow catchers turned to focus on us.

We were forced to slow again as our strength was no longer enough to force so many back when they pressed in as a group. I hacked and slashed at some of them in frustration, but cheers and battle cries from behind us made me glance back.

The change in movement from the demons gave our second group some room to move and press on themselves, and Kryos was able to lead them into using the advantage. They joined us, taking out a significant portion of the creatures between us and them before the handler could instruct his minions to switch their focus.

It was a relief to diminish the enemy so much in such a short space of time, but more were coming. No matter how many of these creatures we killed, there were always more.

Not letting myself grow negative again, I focused on pushing. I used the magic from the entire group to give strength to our weary limbs and charge all the weapons, armor, and shields I could.

As we fought on, we reached the disks we had thrown

earlier. Neritas grinned at me as he snatched his from the air and reached for mine as well. During a gap in the fighting, I took mine from him and charged up both sets again, making sure they would fly well.

Neither of us threw them yet. The path to our intended target was still blocked.

"Alitas, cover Scarlet," Neritas called, barely loud enough for anyone to hear over the shrieks of the demons and the sounds of our dragons fighting.

I frowned, not sure what he intended me to do, but as soon as Alitas shifted to bring his shield in front of my body and move ahead, Neritas dropped his shield and sword at his feet and grabbed me around the waist.

"Jump," he said, his mouth now right by my ear.

I didn't hesitate, trusting him and finally understanding what he was trying to achieve. As he launched me into the air and held me there for a few seconds, I threw the disks I was holding toward the handler.

His eyes widened in surprise, but my aim was a little off. Not ready for the tactic, I had thrown them too soon. They hit a shadow catcher in front of him, and the monster stopped them from thudding into the rotten ground and being lost to us forever.

"Try again with mine." Neritas handed me the second set of disks as soon as my feet were on the ground again.

I took a moment to compose myself. Alitas and Flick fought ahead of us and we were in the middle of the leading group. As soon as I gave Neritas the nod, his body tensed, ready to throw me into the air and keep me up as long as possible.

This time I didn't throw right away, trusting Neritas to

hold me steady while I pumped my magic into him to help him. The handler was more prepared, but we were so close and my throw was aided by magic. The disks hit him in the shoulder.

The lightning that ran through him took his control away from his minions instantly. It was chaos for a moment as they shrieked and stopped moving and fighting. Our dragons took advantage of it and killed several more. Neritas picked his shield back up, and I threw myself at the last few monsters between me and the handler, using the magic I channeled to speed my body up and attack with even more force than normal. The handler wasn't entirely stopped by the disks, somehow managing to lift his arm and pull them from his body.

I fought off another shadow catcher with my attention divided and my mind trying to process the handler saving himself in a way his predecessors hadn't. They hadn't been dumb brutes in the past—they were handlers, each responsible for hundreds of shadow catchers for a reason. But this was the first one who had withstood the pain and damage of the disks long enough to pull the weapon out of himself and attempt to use it against us.

He threw them at me, and, not sure if it would hurt me, I tried to connect to the disks. They felt different and I was pretty sure he had charged them up with magic of another kind. I tried to suck it out, but they were hurtling through the air too fast.

It seemed to resist my pull and I was sandwiched too closely with the dragons I was fighting beside to dodge without disks hitting someone else or me getting in the way and putting another dragon in danger.

With no other choice, I lifted my shield, letting them hit it. I expected them to bounce off and fall into the rot, but they didn't. They embedded in the metal surface and I felt them draining some of the magic from the shield, pulling on my connection as well.

I tried to reach up to pull them out, but they burned my fingers as if they were shadow catchers.

Growling my anger, I left them there and blocked another tail swish that had been meant to catch me off guard. It barely connected with the shield, but it drained it even more and I couldn't seem to charge it back up. The connection took my energy but didn't make the shield any stronger.

Already tired and having put a lot of energy into the pillars, I was forced to draw on the energy of the dragons around me again. They were already providing so much, but this handler wasn't making it easy for us to get to safety and he was holding back, forcing us to fight through his minions to get to him.

Now that he wasn't being hurt by our ranged attacks, the handler was in control once more. The monsters attacked with extra ferocity, bunching in toward me and Neritas again.

Alitas came to my rescue a couple more times as I kept my focus on the handler and tried to get to him. Our group had almost entirely stalled out. I felt for the magic around me, trying to discern if boosting any particular dragons could help us gain the advantage again.

"I'm not sure how much longer I can keep up fighting, healing the land around us, and helping push forward," Neritas said through gritted teeth.

I nodded and exhaled, automatically giving him a little more energy. At the same time, I checked on the levels of all the other green dragons. They were draining fast, and I was only drawing a little from them.

Despite how tough this battle was, we were seeing fewer and fewer shadow catchers, and the numbers that had swarmed us were growing thinner, with few reinforcements behind them.

Considering my options, I decided to go for one big push. Using the magical energy from my sword and the dragons who still had the most to give, I charged the weapons of everyone fighting, also the ground, working outward from where I stood.

The creatures thrashed as the ground underneath them grew green and healthy. It wasn't enough to kill the shadow catchers, but it distracted them and made them shriek and stop attacking. The dragons with me were mostly skilled enough to take advantage of it, although I had to concentrate and could do little more than keep my shield up and stab forward.

Neritas, Alitas, Flick, and Ben soon had the area around me clear, and I walked forward onto the healthy ground. I grabbed the first set of disks I'd thrown and charged them and filled them with as much power as I could muster while I hurried forward. I handed Neritas' disks back to him.

The dragons behind me roared battle cries as they took on the last of the monsters in the circle of rot and gave one final push.

The handler had looked confident before and had been

able to keep himself out of the fighting, but now he snarled and turned to flee.

As soon as he put his back to us, Neritas threw his disks. I ran on as the disks hit their target, crackling in the demon's back. He thrashed, still strong enough not to go down immediately when hit by the weapons, but it stopped him in his tracks long enough that I could catch up.

Thrusting my sword straight through his back, I finished him off. He took a little longer than the shadow catchers to become nothing but smoke, but he was dealt with, and the shadow catchers all stalled again, even the ones farther out from us.

"Time to go," I yelled, just about holding the area with my magic so the whole group could join me.

It had taken a lot of the remaining magic the group possessed, but it had been worth it.

No one needed telling twice to run for the tree line and the relative safety it represented, and I led the charge beside Neritas once more.

With very little to fight for the first time in about two hours, we could make some serious progress, and only the green dragons needed to use any magic. I funneled them what they needed from the rest of us. If they stopped being able to control their powers, we were all doomed.

It took most of the rest of our reserves, and I even had to pull some from the sword I carried to make sure Neritas had a powerful enough flow. His job was harder than the task of those behind him. While they just had to keep the plants healthy, Neritas had to encourage them to grow.

Within another ten minutes, we were back on healthy ground. A few more honor guards were waiting for us. I wasn't sure what they were doing there, but their faces were concerned.

Before any of them could speak, I paused to check what I felt. So close to the gate, it was hard to tell what lurked where, but now that we were beyond its direct reach, I could feel them a little better. More monsters were pouring in from the north and south, far more than we could fight. On top of that, I was pretty sure another handler was nearby.

"We need to get out of here. And fast."

Alitas heard my words as the honor guards tried to get his attention.

"We can't linger," he echoed my sentiment. "We'll have to use the tunnels."

I nodded. I had not wanted Grigick to know about them, but Capricia did, and protecting lives was more important than keeping secrets. We would use the old tunnels to get past the demons.

CHAPTER TWENTY-SIX

Alitas took the lead now, as my powers were best used to monitor the monsters chasing us and make sure no one lagged from weariness. Many of us sported injuries again, but none as bad as our previous attempt to reach the gate. The group was at least learning to fight better as a unit.

We'd only gone a couple hundred yards down the path toward the parking lot and the fork that took us to the tunnels when I heard voices ahead and the helicopters coming back.

This time three circled overhead.

I growled. Now wasn't the time to have humans watching us or getting in the way. Our magic was too low and we focused on getting out of there safely.

"What's got you two looking so agitated? You said the farmhouse is safe." Alitas asked the honor guards who'd come up to meet us now that everyone was on the move again.

"The area the gate influences. It's no longer a complete circle. On the northwest edge, there's a… protuberance."

The words fell on me like a bucket of cold water, making me shudder. That wasn't a good sign. Thankfully not many had heard it, as the group had spread out as we hurried along the path. I didn't doubt the news would travel, though.

My gaze met Alitas', and I hoped he got the message to drop it for now. Whether he did or not, no one said anything else, and the noise ahead caught our attention. A group of hikers was on the path.

"It's around here—" The guy in front stopped when he spotted us jogging. No shadow catchers were attacking us yet, but they were going to be with us soon, still too many for us to fight.

"Get out of here. You're all in danger." I moved to the front of the group as Alitas frowned.

We were forced to stop, losing time. The newcomers didn't react right away but stopped and blocked our route.

It was only as I got closer that I recognized several of them. They were the hikers we had saved several months ago who had sworn secrecy about what they had seen.

"What are you doing here?" I demanded. Alitas had the group behind us form defensive positions and he urged the humans to at least stand inside our shields. It was a decision I responded to kindly. I didn't want them hurt either.

"We came looking for you. We want to help."

"With what?" I asked, so stunned at the stupidity of such an act that I couldn't keep the anger from my voice. They carried no weapons, and none of them had been trained.

"You're fighting evil," one of the women explained. I

could have facepalmed. "We want to help you and protect our planet too."

Alitas came up to them and assessed them. "We don't have weapons to hand you here, and we're low on the capacity to make them effective, but if you can stick with us, we might be able to get you suited up. But you'll have to move fast, do as you're told, and let us keep you safe."

I thought some of them might object, but they simply nodded and Alitas didn't wait to get us moving again. The shadow catchers had gotten a lot closer to us, and we still had some distance to go to the tunnels if I correctly remembered where the entrance was.

My concern grew worse as I noticed the expression on Alitas' face. His jaw was set and he kept glancing at the group behind to check that we were all keeping up. One of the advantages I had of being connected to everyone magically was that I could feel roughly where they were. I knew that most were keeping up, but only because we weren't having to fight and the strongest could help the most vulnerable.

Once more I worried for the elder dragons and their ability to cope with everything being asked of them, but with the magic strength of all of us so diminished I didn't dare use any to help them.

We'd only gone another hundred yards or so when the shadow catchers caught up to us. The path had taken us away from the demons, but they could move faster than us and had caught up to the back end of the group.

Without a moment of hesitation, I stepped up to defend our group and let the vulnerable get to safety. I had said I would be part of the honor guards for this mission, and that meant protecting everyone.

"Ben, lead everyone to the tunnel. Can you remember where it is?"

He nodded but opened his mouth to object. I didn't give him time to respond before I moved to defend us and hold the path. Neritas, Flick, and Alitas came with me, which didn't surprise me.

Ready to take on some demons, I let go of the weakest dragons and stopped drawing magic from them. I drew power and got into place slower than I wanted. The path was narrow and trees were in the way, but the people who had joined us hurried after Ben and Griffin, and several green dragons who had been weakened entirely headed that way too.

Capricia encouraged Brenta past me next, but she hung back herself, lifting her shield and what was left of her sword to fight. Grigick hesitated, but I saw the pained look in his eyes.

"Go on," I suggested. "I think we all know you're not what you hoped to be, but thank you for trying and doing what you could."

It was the kindest way I could think to tell him that he had failed. But he shook his head.

"There's a little strength left in me yet. I can help more, especially if you stand to fight as well."

For the first time since he had tried to claim the throne, he made me believe he'd be an asset and not a liability. The determined look on his face was more genuine than any he'd given before. Maybe he would do credit to his potential after all.

Without the blessing of the ancestors, he was never going to come close to wielding the level of power I did, but at least he was learning. I could work with that.

Most of the honor guards stuck around, but they let me pass and fought alongside me instead of getting in my way and hindering me from getting to the fight.

As the shadow catchers reached me, I threw myself into battle and fought with everything I had left. We had to buy enough time for the rest of the dragons to get into the tunnels and get partway down them before we retreated. My mother was soon close by as well, Reijo not leaving her side.

Full of blood lust toward these monsters, Jace, Cios, Tim, and Harriet fought on like they were possessed, and we formed a strong fighting unit. Despite our collective experience and skill, though, I felt our magic draining. Every attack and block dissipated energy into damage.

While it was needed and we did well overall, it still wore us down, and it was all under the watchful eye of the news helicopters hovering nearby.

I couldn't let them distract me, but I was sure one of them had followed our other group, the humans with us no doubt drawing their attention. The rest stayed focused on me, moving when I did and hovering when I stopped to fight another monster.

Once the vulnerable members of our group had put a little distance between us and them, I encouraged everyone to slowly fall back, slipping out of ranks and down to the end of the line every time the battles were dealt with and another shadow catcher died.

It allowed us to slowly retreat. The monsters were too

fast for any of us to turn and run, but we weren't getting far enough or killing them fast enough to diminish their numbers before more arrived. I was going to have to buy everyone some room to flee once more.

When I found myself at the back of the group, holding the line and feeling the lowest number of creatures close to us since the fight began, I pulled almost all of the magic left from everyone, the weapons I carried, and even the few other weapons and shields the others were wielding that could store magic energy.

Almost bursting with pent-up energy, I charged the ground around us all again and along the path.

"Run," I yelled as I held it safe for all of them.

I retreated as well, not holding the charge of the ground once it fell too far behind me, but charging it up ahead just in case. The shadow catchers were prevented from following too fast.

None of the magical energy was wasted even after I let go of it. It remained on the ground until the demons came over it, the damage being done to the shadow catchers as they moved across the charged ground. Even with a handler nearby urging the monsters onward, they were reluctant to give chase when they were getting hurt.

The strategy was effective but draining, and I couldn't keep it up for long. As I ran, I narrowed the area charged behind me and to the sides. Clever demons would find it easier to get to us, but I got the feeling that they were struggling against their controller and too injured to be entirely obedient.

With everyone running hard for the tunnels, I expected us to catch up to the others and have to stand and defend again, but we were near and our companions were already heading inside.

Grateful for every dragon who had fought alongside me and given it their best, I did everything I could to hold the line a little longer, drawing on all the magic inside me and the thin connection I still felt to the island to the east.

It didn't provide me with magic swiftly, but it helped a little. The slight delay in the pursuit of our foe gave us the last bit of time we needed to get all the vulnerable into the tunnels and for the rest of us to run the last fifty meters or so to reach them.

"Head inside. Don't wait," I called out when I felt many of them slow and consider stopping. I had only a small amount of magic left and almost everyone else was empty when I stopped charging the ground. I'd managed to get to the tunnels and we'd opened up a ten-yard gap between us and our enemy, but it would be eaten fast if our fighters didn't hurry deeper into the dark.

Thankfully, they listened. Jace, Alitas, and Kryos encouraged more and more of them to run down the tunnel. Grigick was out of magic and stumbled a couple of times, having used more after I drew some without completely depleting him, but he made it and somehow lit his sword faintly to give the dragons a little light. It was enough for someone to find a flashlight and get moving while I was forced to pause by the door.

Everyone moved as fast as they could now, but we bottlenecked by the entrance. The demons came closer and closer while I could do nothing but stand between Neritas and Flick and wait for the way to be clear. Alitas and my mother hung back too, but I saw how tired they all were. I couldn't push them any further.

We ran as soon as we could, but the shadow catchers were so close that even when I stepped inside and Alitas got the door shut, they continued to come at it. I used a little more of the remaining energy in the sword to charge the door. With any luck, it would hold them off long enough that the handler gave up.

The dragons ahead were running, taking the flashlights with them and my mother held a glowing stick up so the rest of us could see. It would use more magic but it was a small price to pay for being able to see.

Even as we put distance between us and the monsters, they continued to throw themselves at the door. I swore and wondered how long the charge on the door would last with so many shadow catchers trying to drain it.

There was little I could do if I wanted to protect everyone, however. We needed to get back to the cars and this was the only way to get everyone safe.

Already the more vulnerable were racing ahead of us down the tunnels, the honor guard helping them along the best they could, and even most of the dragons who had fought alongside me were fleeing, but I didn't move from near the door.

The charge was fading and I knew it wasn't going to buy enough time. I had to do something. But I didn't know what else to do. I was so low on magic that I could barely light up my sword to see and there was only a little extra in it to make sure it wouldn't break when I hit a demon with it. The shield was depleted and I slung it on my back again. The disks still stuck out of it, thankfully not drawing any more power from anything and seemingly dormant themselves.

"What are you thinking?" Neritas asked, noticing I was staring at the door and not following my mother and everyone else down the tunnels.

"We need to do something more. Or we won't get away. But we're out of magic. Or at least, close enough to out of magic." I was drawing on my connection to the ancestors and their island to pull in more, but it was like trying to fill up a swimming pool with a dripping faucet.

It wouldn't do much against an army of demons this large. And I could sense another handler somewhere.

"We just need to get far enough down the tunnel and collapse it on them," Neritas said. "If you can give me a little more magic, I can get the trees of the forest to do it."

I exhaled. It would take this escape route away from us permanently, but we had to try something. I nodded, even if I wasn't sure it would work.

Not giving me time to think about it, Neritas took my hand and pulled me down the tunnel. I held the sword out in front of us to light the way, barely able to see Alitas up ahead where the honor guard was making sure everyone else got away safely. Now and then I could make out Flick ahead of him, frequently looking back to see where I was.

It reminded me that more than a few dragons regularly risked their lives for no other reason than they cared about me. They'd followed me a long way and into and out of many dangers.

For now, however, I was protecting them. And that was how it was going to stay.

CHAPTER TWENTY-SEVEN

We were only about a quarter of the way down the tunnels when the shadow catchers broke through the door, rotting it away. They came pouring down the tunnel, gaining on all of us. I was far enough away that we had time to react, but I'd caught up to the main group. None of us were able to travel any faster than the slowest.

Without magical aid, many of the weakest dragons were barely running.

"How long do you need?" I asked Neritas when I felt so many of the monsters entering the tunnel after us and more coming across the surface. It was as if they could follow it now that it had demons inside it.

"Only a minute or two," he replied, still leading me and holding my hand tightly.

I let everyone carry on without hindrance and without telling them that they were being hunted again. No one would go any faster by being scared that we couldn't get away.

We carried on a little longer until the monsters had

closed about half the distance between us and we were halfway through the tunnel. We still had a long way to go and I didn't dare wait any longer.

"Okay, here." I stopped and pulled on Neritas' grip.

He nodded and I connected to his magic again, funneling almost all the magic I had into him. I hadn't built up much, but he had a little left and knew how to channel it best. I pulled almost everything that was left in the sword as well, leaving it good for only one or two more hits. Enough to defend me if a monster got too close, but only so I could run again.

We'd never been this depleted and had so many of the demons so close, but I hoped we could slow them long enough that the rest of the dragons could get into cars and drive away.

As Neritas weakened and slipped to one knee, I felt all the magic in him almost dissipate completely, but the work wasn't complete.

"Don't suppose you've got any more juice stored up somewhere, do you?" he asked. "I've not broken through enough yet."

As I gave Neritas everything I could, he took control of the two nearest trees, both of them large but still growing larger. He deliberately grew the roots down toward us in various places, trying to break through the walls and collapse them inward.

I frowned as it still didn't appear to work, the bricks giving a little, but not enough.

"The ceiling just won't give. The walls are toast," he said as the first few roots came through and started to push bricks out, making it clear he was telling the truth.

As he wobbled again, I put a hand on his shoulder.

"Stop. You need to be able to move again." I helped him to his feet and gave him the tiniest amount of magic to make sure he could at least take the next few steps.

"But it's not done."

"It's okay. I can finish this, but you might want to stand back." I didn't look him in the eyes as I spoke, knowing what I had to do. We were out of magic and I had to protect them. I could only think of one way to make sure they all got away.

Before Neritas could think to do anything other than follow my suggestion, his eyes fixed on me but his trust guided his feet, and I pulled the very last bit of magic from the shield.

It wasn't enough to finish what Neritas had started, but it was enough to charge the sword up one last time.

I took all of the rest of the magic from deep inside me and my connection to the ancestors and poured it into my muscles. I jumped, lunging at the section of tunnel ceiling between the trees where the walls were weakest.

My sword was sharp enough and the magic gave it enough extra bite to dive deep into the large slab above. The slab cracked but nothing else happened for a moment. My sword was wedged, and gravity tried to bring us all back down again. I hung, a foot or so off the ground, held up by the sword and the strength of the tunnel.

Behind me, Neritas was yelling something I didn't understand and running back toward me, and the pack of shadow catchers was in front of me. Too weak to call on any more magic, I had only one option to try.

Wriggling my legs and grabbing the hilt with both

hands. I tried to twist and dislodge the slab itself. At first, I feared I would run out of time, or that I would get the sword loose but still not collapse the tunnel. In the end, neither happened.

"Scarlet, what are you doing?" I heard Neritas yell as the slab gave way and dropped me to the floor.

I had just enough time to fling my body toward Neritas and try to twist away from the slab before everything else collapsed and the side walls gave way a fraction of a second later.

Pain flared as I hit the ground and debris, bricks, and dirt rained down on me. I held the sword out in front of me with one hand and locked eyes with Neritas, but he was still several yards away with a flashlight in his hands. With my legs trapped and more dirt and bricks falling, I reached back to grab my shield.

It was still strapped to my back and resisted my attempts to free it, but I managed to pull it up far enough to cover my head.

"Run," I yelled at Neritas, as the cave-in spread. I powered the shield as much as I could, mostly drawing on the connection I had to the ancestors. My own magic was depleted, and I hoped it would be enough.

Dirt soon covered me, blocking out the light and taking Neritas from view as well. My body was trapped beneath stone and dirt and I couldn't move, but I felt outward and back with my mind, trying to sense the demons. The speed at which they had been hurtling toward me had significantly lessened.

I relaxed for a moment, noting they had now all stopped. Even the monsters on the surface were no longer tearing onward. Their connection to the demons in the tunnels had guided them through the forest above, and now that I'd somehow taken that away, they had all frozen.

While they were trying to get out of the load of dirt and bricks I'd rained down, I had to face that same problem. I hoped I hadn't buried Neritas alive as well. As soon as I thought the words, it started to sink in that I was buried. Under a mound of dirt and rubble. And I had no idea if I could get myself out.

Not sure what else to do to save myself or if I even could be saved, I felt out for the connections to any dragons nearby.

Relief washed through me when I found Neritas fairly near and upright. I hoped that meant he was safe. I had some idea of how far I was away from him, and it helped push back the fear threatening to overwhelm me.

I tried not to think about how much air I had and if it might run out. I had to get out of there before the shadow catchers and their handler figured out that I was buried and vulnerable.

I pulled as much magic from my connection with the ancestors as possible and pushed most of it into the sword and shield. If nothing else, I knew I would have easy access to it, and although I wasn't putting in much, it gave me a task to focus on.

As soon as that was happening automatically, I started wriggling the sword back and forth and moving my arm, trying to pack the dirt around my arm and weapon to the sides and compress it to give myself more space.

It worked, though not as well as I had hoped. More importantly, no more dirt fell in when I moved. I still couldn't move most of my body, and I was wary of moving too much when the shield over my back and head was the only thing keeping the dirt and debris from burying me alive.

Before long, I was exhausted. Even moving a little under such enormous weight was enough to drain my body of what little strength it had left. I wanted to scream and hope someone heard and rescued me, but I didn't dare in case the monsters came to me as quickly as the dragons.

The shadow catchers could technically move through objects if they wished. I had seen one go through a door more than once. But I had also seen them avoid going through an object. And not one of them was moving through the dirt right now. Those I'd buried were seemingly stuck.

I felt the connection to Neritas grow stronger and closer bit by bit, and more connections appeared. I couldn't tell exactly who they all were, but I was pretty sure Alitas and Flick were there. Knowing they were trying to reach me gave me mixed feelings. Now that the tunnel system was weakened, it could cave in on them too.

But I couldn't tell them not to try and save me. And I wasn't sure I'd want to. I didn't think I was easily going to get myself out, but if they weren't giving up on me, I wasn't either.

Still wriggling, I tried to widen the area around me by pushing up lightly on one edge of the shield to see what happened. A little dirt shifted, but it also gave some so I could hold the shield higher.

Hoping I was gaining air as well as space, I did my best to keep moving. Time became meaningless as I worked and pulled in all the magic I could. The shadow catchers pulled back, and the presence of the trapped creatures grew weaker as the rest returned to the gate.

By the time I could move my arm in and out of the space it had previously occupied, I thought I could see a small patch of light beyond and above. Because of how I had positioned the shield, I couldn't see where it was coming from, but it gave me hope that I could get enough air if nothing else.

As more time went on, I couldn't stay entirely calm. I was still unable to move most of my body more than a fraction, and although I'd pulled in a little magic, I didn't have enough to break myself out of my mud coffin. I couldn't even transform, knowing that my body would be half-filled with the mud around me. My only consolation was knowing I had stopped the shadow catchers and taken a bunch of them down with me.

Every other thought was terrifying. I almost wished it had killed me at one point, rather than trapping me underground, especially when I felt some of my friends still standing a little way off. They weren't giving up on me but I couldn't tell them I was alive or exactly where I was. All I could do was keep connected and hope Neritas, Flick, and Alitas could feel that I was there, even if they couldn't see me.

When I dared, I fed each one of them a little bit of magic, hoping it would let them know I was alive. If I was going to get out of there, I would have to rely at least partly on their help.

I never gave up moving and wriggling. Slowly, I managed to shift the dirt and rubble around me and free the upper half of my body well enough that I could work on the lower half. Now and then my movements made more dirt move, however, and it had me worried that if I wasn't careful I really would bury myself.

I lost all track of time as I lifted my torso slowly, letting go of my sword for now and propping myself on one arm to push the shield up and out. I eventually found a section of the wall had fallen over my way, and if I scooped some of the dirt around it and pushed it out, I could make a bigger space.

A couple of times, dirt shifted into the bottom of my space, almost burying the sword, but I was quick to grab it again. I continued to work to make the area big enough that I could pull my legs out of the space behind and get into a cramped crouch under my shield. My legs didn't want to budge at first. I wriggled each one back and forth as I had my hands, widening the gap and compacting the dirt on either side and above.

By the time I had done this a little with both legs, I was tired and had to pause to rest. I didn't rest for long. I could sense Neritas and Flick moving more on the other side. It seemed as if they might have gotten a little closer, but I couldn't be sure.

Eventually, I was in a crouched position and could sit down under the shield and take stock. Now I could move a little and had a space that didn't seem in imminent danger of collapsing on me, I managed to calm down.

Being in a better position and getting out were still two very different achievements, though. Having some magic restored to me also helped. I didn't feel the fatigue of having my magical energy reserves depleted. But I was feeling hungry and thirsty and I had nothing to relieve either issue.

Neither panicked me. I knew I could survive quite a while without food, but if I was in here too much longer without water, dehydration was likely to cause issues.

Neritas and Flick had come closer, and I felt my mother and others in the tunnel ahead as well. I did not doubt that they were terrified, so I connected to my mother and fed her some of the magic I'd stored in my sword to get her attention. Within a second she was sending some back and confirming she'd picked up on it.

A moment later I thought I heard the muffled sound of cheering. It was a relief. They knew I was alive and they were looking for me.

With this spurring me on, I used my sword as a spade, digging forward and packing the dirt and stone tightly behind me. I kept my shield up and against the ceiling, hoping to keep the roof stable as I moved forward.

The dragons on the other side started to dig toward me and we made it bit by bit. I paused several times when I began to feel dizzy and lightheaded. When I moved a little further and dug in with the sword again, I noticed the only light source was the sword I was lighting gently.

Somewhere along the way I had cut off my air supply.

CHAPTER TWENTY-EIGHT

As my mind swam, I fought to keep digging. I felt my friends getting closer to me, but still several feet away. I didn't have a choice now. I had to get to them before I ran out of air, or at least give them the best chance to get to me.

My limbs became heavy and each dig forward with my sword got slower and slower. I tried to push through the heavy feeling as I had pushed through the attack when approaching the gate, but no amount of counting seemed to help.

I paused, the pain in my head and lungs building as I gasped for air. As the oxygen ran out, my breathing grew more rapid, more desperate. Not sure what else to do, I pulled all the magic I'd stored in the sword and shield back into me, trying to ease the ache in my arms and get them moving.

Just a little farther, I told myself.

My head cleared a little, the magic giving my mind enough clarity to keep drawing in more magic, and hope.

Without thinking, I drew some in from the dragons outside as well, trying to take it evenly.

As if sensing my need, my mother thrust my way, and a fraction of a second later I felt a new connection, even more coming my way from that source. With what was left of the combined magic of all of the dragons fueling me, I managed to carry on and somehow calm down.

My chest tightened as I worked, but I wasn't passing out and my limbs worked well enough to keep digging. More debris was dislodged and the shield saved me from being buried again more than once.

I didn't stop.

I couldn't afford to.

Despite all the extra magic coming my way, the supply soon ran out, and the dragons on the other side grew even weaker than me as I tried to suck in enough to keep alive. Having just enough sense to let go of the connections I was using, I paused again.

The magic kept coming, however. It could only have been Grigick and my mother. No one else knew how to push magic out of themselves, and no one else had given up trying to help either.

Exhausted, I stopped, my body collapsing as the air ran out.

I couldn't breathe.

The light in my sword went out, plunging me into darkness as I lay in the dirt. I blinked a few times, not sure if time was passing or not, unable to hear even my gasps, only a buzzing that wouldn't stop.

Instead of darkness and nothing, I noticed the dirt. It

was dark, but I picked out bits of brick and stone in it. Some of it was the same color as the tunnel walls.

The color contrast grew even brighter, the edge of my shield was suddenly visible, and then the full length of my sword. I blinked a few more times as the buzzing slowly faded, replaced by the sound of breathing.

My breathing.

This was followed by voices. The words didn't make sense, but I was no longer alone. My head began to clear, the magic still coming in from at least one source, although slower now and more controlled.

As more seconds ticked by, I could make out the voices more clearly.

"Scarlet? Are you okay?" Alitas called, his tone full of concern.

I shifted a hand as I opened my mouth. No words came out, but more dirt trickled down the side of the shield.

"She's alive, but be careful. There's not a lot holding this section up." My mother was nearby. Although she sounded calm, I could feel her panic. We were still connected, and her magic was as drained as mine.

As my mind cleared more, I found the strength to move again. My shield was still over my head, forming a dome that kept me from being buried entirely.

I pushed it up a little higher again as I tried to shift and get back into a crouch. Dirt fell off my clothes and more shifted around me.

"Careful, Scarlet," Alitas warned again as he came even closer.

I didn't listen, able to see the stream of light coming in from their section of the tunnel. Someone was holding up a flashlight and shining it through the gap they had created. Flick, Neritas, Kryos, and at least one other dragon were digging at the mound of rubble that kept us apart, and other dragons moved behind them.

Alitas was near the opening as if he was contemplating trying to crawl through it to get to me. It wasn't wide enough yet and they were fighting the walls and ceiling wanting to give way more. When he saw me holding up a section with my shield, Alitas called more of the honor guards forward. They used their shields and bodies to do the same, forcing the area to stabilize by using the magic left in their equipment.

I dug toward them, trying to widen the hole from my end and dig up toward them. Feeling weak, I was grateful for the magic Grigick was providing, but when he ran out I stumbled. I was still trapped for now.

"You okay, Red?" Neritas asked.

"As okay as I can be trapped on the other side of a cave-in," I replied, almost surprised to find my voice worked.

"You did cause it."

"I think you started it."

"Fair. Although you commanded it."

"So because I'm your queen, it's my fault if the plan doesn't work?" I asked, grinning despite my predicament.

"That is how leadership works, Your Highness," Alitas replied. "When you have made a plan that goes well, everyone who carried it out for you will be praised. When it fails, you will be blamed."

"At least I know what I'm getting myself into." By the time I finished speaking, the hole was wide enough and low enough that I could reach through and pass my sword out.

Alitas took it and handed it to Ben. He passed it back and a group of hands reached through to take hold of me. I kept my shield over my head, hoping it would fit through the gap with me, and put my arm in theirs. With so many of them helping, they soon pulled me through the gap.

I held my breath and closed my eyes, dirt covering my face again for a few seconds before I was out on the other side with them.

Neritas grabbed me first, his strong arms pulling me in against him as someone took the shield away from me.

"Okay, everyone not holding the walls up, fall back to a safer section." Alitas took charge, ever my protector. At least when he knew what madcap ideas I was having.

Whether I wanted to move or not, I was practically hauled down the tunnel by Neritas. Flick put an arm around me from the other side to make sure I didn't resist.

I didn't have the strength, even if I'd had the desire, and I leaned on them both more than ever.

Near the back of the group, her eyes wide with a worry that turned to relief when she saw me, stood my mother. Reijo's arm was around her, her body so drained of magic that she couldn't support herself.

Now that we were in a safer section of the tunnel, Neritas and Flick let me slow enough for us to hug.

"Thank you," I whispered, knowing how much it had cost her to keep the magic flowing.

"I've never had a chance to be there for you. Today I did what any mother would have."

I turned my head, scanning for the other red dragon

who'd helped me, even if only in a very limited way, but Grigick was not among the faces I could distinguish. Before I could say anything else, I was swept on again. The honor guard needed to get clear, and everyone was eager to get out of the tunnel. I couldn't blame them, and I let them pull me along.

It took a while to get to the exit, and we didn't rush now that nothing was pursuing us. Everyone else was waiting in the large room near the exit. Safe underground, but in a much more reinforced area with more light and space.

Most of them looked relieved when they saw us all safe and sound, and Griffin even cheered. I stopped leaning on Flick and Neritas, feeling stronger and not wanting any of the others to see how close I had come to dying. Grigick was one of the first to move, following Jace, who clapped me on the back.

"You're insane, Red, but I'll give you credit. You get the job done."

I grinned and focused on my rival. He'd helped keep me alive with more magic coming from him than anyone else. With all of his posturing, very little had been used from him and he had plenty to give still.

"I think I understand now why so many of these dragons are willing to follow you. You do not ask of them anything you're not willing to do yourself. And you are clearly willing to lay down your life to protect us all, whether we follow you or not." Grigick nodded at me and got down on one knee. "I will give you my support to be crowned our queen at the first available opportunity. I withdraw my claim to the throne."

"Grigick!" Brenta snapped as she shot to her feet.

Capricia put out a hand and stopped the elder from coming over to us. She shook her head and looked at me.

"You've got guts, Red." Capricia got down on one knee as well.

The dragon next to her did the same, and the next, until everyone but Brenta was kneeling before me. I gulped, not sure what would happen now. I refused to demand that she join in, but she nodded.

"I may not always agree with it, but I know when the will of the people is firmly against me. You have won them over, and so I will try to understand and give way with grace." She went to kneel as well, but her body was so frail and tired that the pain it caused her to try was obvious.

I moved to her and stopped her.

"I'll never ask anyone to give me and our race any more than they are capable of. All I will ask is that people find the value in themselves and their unique talents and their loyalty. We're in this together. All of us want the same goal, to see the world and all its inhabitants thriving and making the best of what we've been given."

Slowly, everyone stood.

Alitas was the first to move, going to the exit and getting several of the honor guards to help him pry it open. It was looser than it had been the first time, but they still had to put some effort in to get it to shift far enough.

Eventually, we all stood in the sunlit afternoon. I finally looked down at my dirt-covered body before reaching up and feeling my hair. More dirt fell out.

I grimaced and glanced up to see Neritas and Flick both grinning at me.

"I look like crap, don't I?"

"We weren't going to say anything." Flick snickered.

"You did almost die." Neritas shrugged, still grinning.

"I believe it's impolite to tell the queen she's not looking her best." Ben smirked and Neritas offered me his arm.

"Clean or not, may I escort you back to your car, Your Highness?"

I rolled my eyes but nodded and took the offered support. For now, I wanted to just go home.

It wasn't a short walk back to the cars, but some of the dragons with more physical strength went ahead and brought the cars back to us.

I slipped into the back of one as the first helicopters came up the road, looking for us. Grateful to be out of view already and sandwiched between Neritas and Flick, I trusted Alitas to get me safely away from here.

But I didn't entirely relax. I felt the gate from here. The presence of the demon behind it was closer to the surface than ever. I had filled the working pillars with as much magic as they could handle, and they would hold for now. But with one of them entirely broken, the gate was weakened in a whole new way.

My work to keep Earth safe had only just begun.

EPILOGUE

My hands shook as I thought about what was going to happen over the next hour. It was surreal. I was about to be crowned, and everyone in Detaris had decided this was a good thing.

It helped when Brenta and Capricia made it clear they supported me. And Grigick had made a pretty speech about learning that sometimes it was better to support another and step out of the driver's seat than demand to be followed when both would achieve the same result. It was a speech I was sure someone else had written, and it had vague hints of what I had told Brenta, Capricia, and Alitas when I had agreed to give Grigick a chance to prove himself.

I wanted the world to be protected. I didn't care if I was in charge or in another role, as long as everyone was helping.

Of course, now I was going to be in charge. I'd considered refusing, but my mom had reminded me that there was no one else, my father had wanted me to rule, and the only other option was Grigick. I didn't have a choice and everyone knew it.

A week had passed since we'd been at the gate and out in the human world. I'd been hiding in Detaris ever since. The human world was obsessed with me now, believing that I really was fighting evil and demons and that I was some special warrior race from old.

They had been looking for me ever since. The road outside Detaris was lined with tents full of people hoping to glimpse me going in and out of the city. Some of the humans tried to come closer, but the magic that held the city hidden from view also deterred them and made it appear as if there was nothing there but a cliff. No one dared to try walking off it.

I tried to breathe deeply as my mother appeared, then Ben, Flick, Neritas, and Alitas.

"Are you ready?" My mother's eyes were bright as she looked at me.

I looked down at the clothes I was wearing, a royal uniform I had never expected to wear: a skirt I didn't feel comfortable in and a top that was far too tight. But I knew to them I looked amazing. My hair had been done, ready to hold the tiara that would be my crown. It was a modified version of the large dragon crown my mother had given me the day we'd met. This smaller one befitted me being crowned in human form.

While I thought about my mother's question, not sure the answer would ever truly be yes, I heard the music start outside.

Detaris was going to crown me their queen whether I was ready or not. And they wanted to celebrate. It was the complete opposite of how they had treated me the first time the elders had suggested I be crowned. But the circumstances couldn't have been worse. The world was in danger and Detaris wanted to throw a party.

Despite my thoughts, I nodded and let Ben take my arm. As my acting guardian, he was walking me and my mother to the throne, Alitas, Flick, and Neritas were our honor guard, one behind each of us.

Once we were lined up and ready to walk out, Alitas leaned forward to whisper in my ear. "We'll talk about the gate as soon as we're through this. Jace said she's got some ideas."

I exhaled. The words were exactly what I needed to hear. I could endure standing on ceremony and letting people ogle for a short while if it meant I could get straight back to work afterward.

THE STORY CONTINUES

The story continues with book six, *Dragon Crowned*, available at Amazon.

Claim your copy today!

ACKNOWLEDGMENTS

This book is another that took me far longer to write than I'd hoped. But write it I did and I hope it still reaches the caliber of writing and storytelling that you, my darling readers, expect of me. I appreciate each and every one of you and the journey you all keep me on. These books are written as much for all of you as they are for me these days and I love nothing more than hearing from you all to say that you've enjoyed them.

I also owe everyone at LMBPN a huge debt of gratitude. These wonderful folks continue to do everything they can to help me and bring the books to you in the best state possible. They care about the details, the story and they care about me and it shows in every element of this process. Thank you Robin, Steve, Kelly, Grace, Tracey, Jacqui and everyone else who helps with these but I don't know by name yet. You're all amazing and you make LMBPN feel like family.

To Bryan, for being there no matter the time of day or night. I've had a lot of healing to do lately and you've been there to hold me and calm me through some of the worst of it. A year or two ago many people told me that I was running away from my problems and that I should stick around to face them. That I was giving up on something worth saving and that the grass wasn't greener on the other side. Respectfully, every single one of them was wrong. You're a big part of the reason the grass really was greener on the other side, and walking away from something that only had the capacity to damage me and trap me in a world I didn't belong in was the right thing to do.

You've shown me what it is to truly be cared for and to care in return. To love wholeheartedly, without agenda, cost or control.

Thank you.

To my tiny humans, for being wonderful little people and showing me adventure in the simple again. You haven't had it easy the last few years either, but you've embraced the new adventurous life I want to show you and helped make it all worthwhile. A lot of the changes I made, I made to hopefully show you both not to settle for something less than who you are and everything you're capable of. I love you both completely and utterly for whoever you grow into being. And I can't wait to discover, support and encourage you every step of the way.

To Bear, Andrew, David, Clare and Anne-Mhairi. I thank all five of you every book because you influence every book in one way or another. You guys keep me going through the bad times, are there to celebrate the good times and accept me for who I am. You're my favorite people and I love seeing all of you shine as well.

And last but not least to God. Because no matter what happens, I have and always will be your child, exploring the world You created and trying to be just like your Son, someone who loves everyone, exactly as they are.

ABOUT THE AUTHOR

Jess is in the process of changing her name. She's been through a difficult year that leaves her wanting a fresh start and a chance to be the person she's always meant to be. Over the next little while all her books will be moving to Talia Beckett and you'll find all future releases under this author name.

Talia was born in the quaint village of Woodbridge in the UK, has spent some of her childhood in the States and now resides near the beautiful Roman city of Bath. She lives with her two tiny humans (one boy and one girl) and near an amazing group of friends who support her career and life choices.

During her still relatively short life Talia has displayed an innate curiosity for learning new things and has therefore studied many subjects, from maths and the sciences, to history and drama. Talia now works full time as a writer and mummy, incorporating many of the subjects she has an interest in within her plots and characters.

When she's not busy with work and keeping her tiny humans alive she can often be found with friends, playing with miniature characters, dice and pieces of paper covered in funny stats and notes about fictional adventures her figures have been on.

You can find out more about the author and her

upcoming projects by joining her on facebook, by watching her live D&D streams, or emailing her via taliabeckettwriter@gmail.com. Talia loves hearing from a happy fan so please do get in touch!

Talia is also opening up her discord for fans to come chat about what she's up to, and see a few sneak peaks of future work. There's also a chance to become one of her beta readers. If you'd like to check that out you can do so here.

CONNECT WITH THE AUTHOR

Connect with Talia

Mailing list [sign up](#)
Facebook [group](#).
Discord [group](#)
Actual play D&D stream: [Twitch](#) or [Youtube](#)
Email address: [contact me here](#).

BOOKS BY JESS MOUNTIFIELD / TALIA BECKETT

Already published

Urban Fantasy

Dragon of Shadow and Air:

Air Bound

Shadow Sworn

Dragon Souled

Earth Bound

Night Sworn

Dryad Souled

Water Bound

Day Sworn

Pegasus Souled

Fire Bound

Light Sworn

Phoenix Souled

Dragon Apparent:

Dragon Missing

Dragon Seeking

Dragon Revealed

Dragon Rising

Dragon Defying

Time of the Dragon (with Andrew Bellingham):
Dragon's Code
Dragon's Inquisition
Dragon's Redemption
Dragon's Revolt

Fantasy

Tales of Ethanar:
Wandering to Belong (Tale 1)
Innocent Hearts (Tale 2 & 3)
For Such a Time as This (Tale 4)
A Fire's Sacrifice (Tale 5)

Winter Series:
The Hope of Winter (Tale 6.05)
The Fire of Winter (Tale 6.1)

Guild of the Eternal Flame:
Wayfarer's Sanctuary
Protector's Secret
Healer's Oath

Other Fantasy:
The Initiate (under Holly Lujah)

Writing with Dawn Chapman:

Jessica's Challenge (#5 in the Puatera Online series)

Dahlia's Shadow (#6 in the Puatera Online series)

Lila's Revenge (#7 in the Puatera Online series)

Sci-Fi:

Fringe Colonies:

Alliance

Haven

Rebellion

Rebirth

Reclamation

Star Trail:

Hunted

Sherdan series:

Sherdan's Prophecy

Sherdan's Legacy

Sherdan's Country

Sherdan's Road (A short story in the anthology 'The End of the Road')

The Slave Who'd Never Been Kissed (A short in the charity anthology 'Imaginings')

New Beginnings

Santa's Little Space Pirate

In the multi-author Adamanta series:

Episode 1 – Adamanta

Episode 3 – Excelsior

Episode 8 – Phoenix

Episode 13 – New Contacts

Episode 17 – Sacrifice

Other:

Clues, Claws and Christmas

Non-Fic:

How to Write Lots, and Get Sh*t Done: the Art of Not Being a Flake

Find purchase links here

Coming soon:

Urban Fantasy:

Dragon Apparent:

Dragon Crowned

Dragon Defending

Dragon Unveiling

Time of the Dragon (with Andrew Bellingham):

Dragon's Summit

Dragon's Reckoning

Fantasy:

(Tales of Ethanar):

The Pursuit of Winter (#2 in the Winter series, Tale 6.2)

Books under Amelia Price

Mycroft Holmes Adventures:

The Hundred Year Wait

The Unexpected Coincidence

The Invisible Amateur

The Female Charm

The Reluctant Knight

The Ambitious Orphan

The Unconventional Honeymoon Gift

The Family Reunion

The Immortal Problem

The Unremarkable Assistant

Coming soon:

Mycroft 11

About the Author

OTHER BOOKS FROM LMBPN
PUBLISHING

Sign up for the LMBPN email list to be notified of new releases and special deals!

https://lmbpn.com/email/

For a complete list of books by LMBPN please visit:

https://lmbpn.com/books-by-lmbpn-publishing/

www.ingramcontent.com/pod-product-compliance
Lightning Source LLC
LaVergne TN
LVHW041223080526
838199LV00083B/2404